Belonging and betrayal...

Bronia's story

A fictional biography
of
Bronisława Wieniawa Długoszowska

Dr. Gervase Vernon

ISBN-13: 978-1482566840
ISBN-10: 1482566842

In Memory of my Mother
Susanna Vernon (Wieniawa-Długoszowska)
only Daughter of
Bronisława Wieniawa Długoszowska

'How poor are those who ask no questions.'
Leopold Staff

ABOUT THE AUTHOR

Dr. Gervase Bolesław Vernon is the grandson of Bronia
(Bronisława Wieniawa Długoszowska.)
Born in Paris he studied medicine in Cambridge
and London. He has worked as a general practitioner
(family Doctor) and as a medical report writer at the
"Medical Foundation for the Care of Victims of Torture"
(Freedom from Torture".) He lives in Felsted, Essex.

Contents

List of Illustrations   vii

Introduction   2

List of characters   4

Family trees   7

Descendants of Salomon Kliatchkin   7

Descendants of Bolesław Długoszowski   9

Descendants of Charles Laurent   10

Belonging and betrayal... Bronia's story   12

Day 1 A summary   12

Day 2 Paris 19104   14

Day 3 Childhood 1886 to 1900   16

Day 4 Moscow 1918, the Witkacy portrait   17

Day 5 About Bolec (1918-1940)   19

Day 5 The same evening, Bolec (1881-1920)   21

Day 6 About spying (1918)   25

Day 7 France 1914-1917   26

Pierre in Russia Petrograd 1916-17   29

Day 8 Petrograd 1917, Bronia as a spy   30

How I freed Bolec 1918   34

Day 9 Moscow 1918, love   37

Day 10 Moscow 1918, first attempt at escape   40

Day 11 Moscow 1918, Bronia's escape   42

Contents *(continued)*

Day 12 About spying and Bronia's false passport   46

Day 13 Exile 1918, Aberdeen   48

Day 14 Exile, London 1918   50

Day 15 Exile, boat to Stockholm 1918   51

Day 16 Exile, Paris 1918   53

Day 17 A blessing   55

Day 18 Warsaw 1920   57

Day 19 Kraków 1920, the birth of Susanna   60

Warsaw 1923 Artur Szyk   62

Bronia's story, Bobowa (summer of 1931)   65

Day 20 Warsaw 1938 The officers' ball   68

Day 21 Rome 1938 - June 1940   72

Day 22 Second exile, America 1940 - 1st July 1942   74

Day 23 Bolec's suicide New York, 1st July 1942   78

Wieniawa's suicide note   82

Police statement of Roberto Smith 1/7/42   83

Day 24 About memory   84

Day 25 About Bolec   86

Day 26 About Leon   87

Day 27 A dream about Paulina   89

Day 28 Bronia's death 1953   90

Timeline for the life of Bronia   93

Sources   94

List of Illustrations

"Portrait of Mrs. Berenson" by Witkacy (Moscow1918)   1

Bronia's false passport and detail   45

Bronia in the Belweder palace, Warsaw (early 1920)   58

"King Casimir III ratifying the "Statutes of Kalisz""
By Artur Szyk (1920)   63

The manor house at Bobowa (circa 1980)   66

The officers' ball (Warsaw 1938)   69

Bolec as ambassador in Rome (1938)   71

Bronia, Bolec and Susanna on board ship to exile
in New York (July 1940)   75

Susanna finds her vocation; interpreting at the UN
(Lake Success 1946)   81

"Portrait of Mrs. Berenson" by Witkacy (Moscow1918)

Introduction

This short work about my grandmother, Bronisława Wieniawa Długoszowska, was written in 2011-12 after my mother Susanna's death. She was Bronia's daughter and her only child. Bronia has left little mark in history although her husband General Bolesław Wieniawa-Długoszowski is well-known in Poland. Eight books about him are listed in the sources. He was the most loyal aide of Marshall Piłsudski, the central figure in the political life of Poland between the wars. But Bronia has been written out of the story for reasons that will become apparent in the text; principally that she was Jewish. Yet her life was no less interesting. She lived in the eye of the storm of twentieth century history and it destroyed her. Although I have included a list of sources at the end, the principal source is my mother. She told me most of these stories, although the telling changed as I grew older.

My mother did hide from us her father's (General Wieniawa's) suicide. My late sister Catherine and I discovered it when I was seventeen. But she did not hide our Jewishness, the nature of the Holocaust, the Warsaw uprising or the halt of Soviet troops before Warsaw; on these matters she was always clear. (The Soviet troops waited on the far side of the Vistula for six months to enable the Germans to crush the Warsaw uprising which might have led to Poland as an independent state rather than a Soviet satellite.)

I wrote this story as an act of grief, but also because it is a good story. So little is known about Bronia that I chose to write a fictional biography. Nevertheless I have tried to be faithful to places and dates where they are known.

I must express gratitude to many people, principally my wife Susan who has, over the years, encouraged me to write down these stories. For the cover and other artwork I am grateful to my friend John Plunkett. The book would never have been written without the help of the writing group at Churchill College, Cambridge, ably led by Rosie Johnston[1]. Bronia's portrait was beautifully restored by Jane McAusland; perhaps Britain's leading conservator of art on paper. Finally, among many people who commented on the initial text, special thanks are due to Alexander Lauterbach, a Polish Jew, originally from Cracow, now eighty nine years old. He survived the Holocaust, escaped to America via Japan and married into the family of Artur Szyk.

Dr. Gervase Vernon
Cambridge/Felsted
January 2013

---

[1] http://www.rosie-johnston.com/

List of characters

Bronisława Wieniawa-Długoszowska, known as Bronia, born 1886, birthplace unknown, died Paris 1953. Baptised Lutheran 1894. Studied medicine in Paris from 1908, nurse at "Le Continental", Paris, September 1914. Name used while working for French military intelligence in Russia "Jeanne-Liliane Lalande". Born Bronisława Kliatchkin, first husband 1909, Moscow, Leon Berenson, second Bolesław Wieniawa-Długoszowski.

General Bolesław Ignacy Florian Wieniawa-Długoszowski, known as Bolec in the family but in Poland as "Wieniawa" (22/7/1881 – 1/7/1942) born Maksymówka, in the Ukrainian part of the Austro-Hungarian Empire (see note 4, p.9), died New York. First wife Stefanią Calvas, second Bronisława. General, politician, poet, diplomat,"President for a day" of the Polish Republic (25/9/1939.)

Susanna Vernon, daughter of Bronia and Bolec, (11/8/1920 - 3/8/2011). Born Krakow, died London. Born Susanna Wieniawa-Długoszowska. Interpreter. Wife of John Vernon (3/8/16 - 15/10/2011)

Pierre Laurent 2/5/1892 – 1/3/1935. Born and died in Paris. Working in Russia 1/11/16 to 2/18 (Petrograd) with the mission of General Lavergne and General Niessel and 6/18 to 11/18 (Moscow) as an undercover agent for the French government. No children.

Leon Berenson 27/7/1882 – 22/4/1941. Born Warsaw and died in the Warsaw ghetto during the German occupation. Lawyer, defence council in the Tsarist courts in Warsaw for socialist and communist activists, including Felix Dzerzhinsky, worked as a legal counsel in

4

the Polish embassy in America in the 1920s. He was a prominent lawyer in Poland in the years between the wars. First husband of Bronisława (Moscow 1909). No children.

Felix Dzerzhinsky 1877-1926 born Ivyanets, Belarus, died Moscow. Early communist and founder of the Cheka (the first Soviet state security force, predecessor of NKVD, KGB, etc.)

Stanisław Ignacy Witkiewicz 24/2/1885 – 18/9/1939, known as "Witkacy". Born Warsaw, committed suicide on 18/9/1939 after hearing of the Soviet invasion of Poland. Painter, playwright, philosopher.

Artur Szyk 16/6/1894 – 13/9/1951. Born Łódź, Poland, died New Canaan, Connecticut, USA. Illuminator and cartoonist.

Violaine Hoppenot, radio-operator in the Belgian resistance during WW2, pseudonym, "Madame Dusoulier", daughter of Henri (1891-1977) French diplomat and Helene Hoppenot (1896-) photographer and writer

Laurent family (Paris); parents Charles Laurent (1856-1939), President of the "Credit National" and Sophie de Benazé, children; Pierre Laurent (1892-1935), Jean Laurent (1894-1916) and Jacques Laurent (1896-1989) husband of Zocia Kliatchkin, Bronia's younger sister.

Kliatchkin family (Moscow); parents Salomon Kliatchkin (КЛЯЧКИН), lawyer, founder of the first Russian credit reference agency, born 1858, died Yalta 28/11/1916 from TB and Helene Bajénoff (Баженов) (later known as Babushka which is the diminutive for grandmother in Russian) died Paris (1868-1945), children; Bronisława (1886-1953), Marie (1887-1937), one of the first women to qualify as a mining engineer (University of Liege 1909) mother of Acia (1923) and Helena (Lily) (1928-), Gregory (1888- died of croup 1890), Adolphe (1891-1973), Sigismund (Zyga) (1893-1937) a lawyer then officer in the artillery, father of Galina (1928-), Guerman (1895-1948) , Officer in the Russian air force, (Marie, Sigismund, Guerman, died in Soviet prisons) Paulina (1897-1976) TB specialist died peacefully in Barnaul, Siberia, Zocia (1899-1987) married Pierre Laurent's brother Jacques, three daughters (Jacqueline, Nicole, Anne), Roma, latterly an orthodox nun (1902-1959), Vera (1909-1999) translator for the European Union. (Roma, Zocia, Adolphe and Vera all died in Paris.)

Wieniawa family; parents Bolesław Długoszowski (senior) (29/11/1843-12/3/1912) (born Lelów died Bobowa), railway engineer and Josephine Struszkiewicz, children; Kazimierz (Kazek) older brother, first wife well-born Viennese, second wife a Polish Gipsy, mother of Leszek, Bolesław (see above), Teophila, mother of Wanda, grandmother of Irena (Inka).

Family trees

Descendants of Salomon Kliatchkin

Salomon Grigorievitch Kliatchkin
Born: 1858 Died: Yalta 28 November 1916
Married: **Helena Yefimovna Kliatchkin (Bajenov)** 1885
Born: 1868 Died: Paris 1945

Bronisława Wieniawa-Długoszowska (Kliatchkin)
Born: 1886 Died: Paris 1953
1st husband; **Leon Berenson**
Born: 27 July 1882 Died: 22 April 1941 Married: Moscow 1909
2nd husband; **General Boleslaw Wieniawa-Długoszowski**
Born: 22 July 1881 Died: 7 January 1942

Susanna Vernon (Wieniawa-Długoszowska)
Born: 11 August 1921 Died: 3 August 2011
Married: **John Vernon**
Born: 3 August 1916 Died: 15 October 2011
Catherine (1950-2008), **Gervase** (1953-), **Teresa** (1959-)

Marie Kliatchkin
Born: 1887 Died in the Gulag 1937?
Married: **Arkady Dlougatch** (lawyer) 1910
shot during Stalin's great purge in 1937
Acia Born: 1923 **Lily** Born: 1928

Gregory Kliatchkin
Born: 1888 Died of croup 1890

Adolphe (Clo-clo) Kliatchkin
Born: 1891 Died: Paris 1973

Sigismund Kliatchkin
Born: 1893 Married: **Dina Makline** (? -1979?)
Shot during Stalin's purge in 1937
Galina Kliatchkin Born: 1925

Guerman Kliatchkin
Born: 1895
Married: **Ekaterina Mitkevitch-Daletzkaia** (?-1949),
no children, Died in the Gulag 1948

Dr. Paulina Kliatchkin
Born: 1897 Died: Barnaul, Siberia 1976

Zocia Laurent (Kliatchkin)
Born: 1899 Died: Paris 1987 Married: 1919
Jacques Laurent
Born: 1896 Died: 1989
Anne Leveque (Laurent)
Nicole De Chavagnac (Laurent)
Deceased
Jacqueline Garnier (Laurent)
Deceased

Romana (Roma) Kliatchkin
Born: 1902 Died: Paris 1959

Vera Kliatchkin
Born: 1909 Died: Paris 1999

Family trees *(continued)*

Descendants of Bolesław Długoszowski

Bolesław Długoszowski
Born: 29 November 1843 Died: Bobowa 12 March 1912
Married: **Josephine Długoszowska (Struszkiewicz)** Deceased

General Bolesław Wieniawa-Długoszowski
Born: 22 July 1881 Died: New York 7 January 1942
1st marriage; **Stefanią Calvas** Deceased
2nd marriage; **Bronisława Wieniawa-Długoszowska (Kliatchkin)**
Born: 1886 Died: Paris 1953
Daughter; **Susanna Vernon (Wieniawa-Długoszowska)**
Born: Krakow 11 August 1920 Died: London 3 August 2011
Married; **John Vernon**
Born: 3 August 1916 Died: London 15 October 2011

Teophila Długoszowska Deceased
Daughter **Wanda**
Granddaughter **Irena Bokiewicz**

Kazimierz Długoszowski Deceased
1st marriage; Viennese noblewoman
2nd marriage; Polish gipsy
Son **Leszek Długoszowski**

Descendants of Charles Laurent

Charles Laurent
Born: 1856 Died: 1939
and **Sophie Laurent (de Benazé)** Deceased

Pierre Laurent
Born: 1892 Died: 1935

Jean Laurent
Born: 1894 Died in battle 1916

Jacques Laurent
Born: 1896 Died: Paris 1989 Married: 1919
Zocia Laurent (Kliatchkin)
Born: Moscow 1899 Died: Paris 1984
Jacqueline Garnier (Laurent) Deceased
Anne Leveque (Laurent)
Nicole De Chavagnac (Laurent) Deceased

Belonging and betrayal...
Bronia's story

If you go up the Mount of Olives near Jerusalem to see the sunrise, you will be surrounded by Jewish fathers holding their babies to their bearded faces and whispering into their ears the story of Israel. What my grandmother Bronisława Wieniawa-Długoszowska (Bronia) is doing in the following pages is whispering her story, her truth, to her baby grandson; a truth that Stalin and Hitler would have suppressed.

Day 1 A summary

Bronia is a lady in her mid-sixties, though she looks older. She is in a room in her flat in Paris. The light is grey; the flat is poorly kept and with little furniture. In her arms she holds her first grandson. As she looks at him a smile breaks out on her face, a face which has not smiled for a long time. She talks to the baby.

Gervase, at last I hold you in my arms. For many years I longed for a son and look, now a grandson. I did not want to rush to see you in hospital. My sister Zocia went. She told me that she could recognise you from the army of babies in the nursery because of your nose. Your long nose was folded over your face. And she was right. I too can recognise you for you have my husband Bolec's nose, which has passed through my daughter Susanna to you. Now that I have seen you I feel ready to go.

Already an old woman at sixty-six, tossed about in the eye of the storm for many years, I am ready to go now. Stranded in this flat between the living and the dead, between Jews and gentiles, I will not resist the time of departure when it comes. All my life I have lived at the margins where the drifting continents collide and splinter.

Look at you, not smiling yet but so content. To you I can tell the truth after a life of lying and dissimulation; an old spy can relax at last and let down her guard to one who cannot hear her, or if he does, will not judge. Be alert, Gervase, do not be taken in by the lies; keep quiet if you must, but remember the truth in your heart. My sister Zocia does not know that she is Jewish; has she forgotten it or did she never know it[2]? But I have always been honest with myself and my daughter Susanna: it is my clear-sightedness that has saved our lives many times. But could I have saved more? Why do I survive myself when so many better people have died? You were born in the American hospital in Paris. The lady in the next bed held her baby up and said; 'This is my victory against Hitler'. But for me it is not as simple as that: my hands are weary and grow cold. Soon I too will be leaving.

Before I set you back in your cot, let me tell you how it started. Until I was eight we were a good Jewish family. We lived in Moscow. We followed all the rituals prescribed by our religion. Only Papa ventured outside into the Gentile world. Then when I was eight we were all baptised into the Lutheran church so that Papa could get the position in Russian society he so greatly deserved. But from that day I learnt to lie. I had to lie at my new school about my origins. I

---

[2] According to Jewish law one is Jewish if one has a Jewish mother

had to lie even though all the other girls knew I was Jewish. But as well as lies I learnt one truth; a truth, my beloved, I want to pass on to you. There is only one God. The God of the Jews is the same as the God of the gentiles. And while Jews and gentiles may have opposite thoughts about almost everything; they are all people. When their children die they mourn, when a husband is unfaithful it is like a knife tearing in the chest. But you, Gervase, you will not be unfaithful to me: your little legs would not carry you away. I put you down in the cot and you will be there when I return. You will not jump off any roof.

Day 2   Paris 1910

A spring day in the "Jardin du Luxembourg" a small public garden in Paris. Bronia is very simply dressed but looks smart. She is holding her grandson Gervase.

Gervase, it's good to hold you again. There are two things I must explain to you; how grandmothers talk to babies and who this grandmother is who is talking. When grandmothers talk to babies they can talk nonsense, they have no inhibitions... It's a bit like a religious person talking in tongues to their God. You talk out of sheer wonderment; there is no need to explain or hide since you are already understood. The second thing is who this grandmother is. She is a wounded grandmother who has been through several cataclysms; you must not expect her to be always rational or right. If she is talking to you about life, it is about the wonder and the pain. The wonder and the pain will be as much in the manner of talking as in what is said.

If I could come back to your nose which is now quite straight and is no longer folded over your face. That nose is already cutting the air hungrily – like the sabre of a cavalry officer. It is your grandfather's, my husband Bolec's, nose. The first time I saw it I was sitting at the café "La Rotonde" on the Chaussée de le Muette in Paris. I was there with my younger sister Paulina and a group of other Russian medical students. We were earnestly discussing religion and politics when a group of Poles strutted past our table. Bolec was in the lead, hands moving like windmills, nose slashing through the Parisian air, mouth open wide in laughter as he led the group. Perhaps my eye paused on him, because Paulina said, 'Now that is exactly the sort of Pole you ought to avoid; they only cause trouble.' I agreed with her; indeed I was already married, but my eyes may have lingered. If Wieniawa turned around to see me, I certainly looked away disdainfully; but then he looked at all the girls.

I must not trouble you with thoughts beyond your age. (Pause.) But he is your grandfather, indeed I love him still. It was many years before I saw him a second time, by which time life had been utterly transformed for us both. He was brave, he was good and generous; he was certainly good-looking. Then, and later, he cast a spell on you: when he looked at you, you thought you were the only person in the room. His attention was total even when it was only brief.
Look at this garden while I tell you about love. This is the garden where, in Victor Hugo's "Les Misérables", Marius falls in love with Cosette. Marius sees her and catches sight of her face but it is months before they exchange a word. So it was with Bolec. In the same way it will be many months before you can reply to me. You already feel comfortable in my arms, lying relaxed as I hold you, I can float away on memories before the pain occurred and life was still pure.

15

Day 3 Childhood 1886 to 1900

Bronia is in her flat. It is midday and light is streaming in.

Gervase, today I think I'll talk to you about my childhood. We are alone, so I'll talk to you in Yiddish, which is what we spoke at home in my early years. Later it was a secret language between me and my parents. The younger children never learnt it, but went straight on to Russian in the nursery. Poor Mummy was always pregnant so we did not see much of her. But when I was young there were plenty of aunts and uncles around. Everybody spoke Yiddish at home, except the Russian servants. The school I went to from the age of five was Russian speaking, but all the pupils were Jewish. So we could speak Yiddish during break times (we were supposed to speak Russian even then, but nobody really told us off). It was a womb-like world; and if Russian children on the way to school shouted at us or threw snowballs we paid no attention.

Then suddenly when I was eight we were all taken off to the Lutheran church to be baptised[3]. Papa did ask us, Maria (then seven) and I, but it was clear to me, even at eight, that it was a question to which we could not answer no. After that we moved to a grander house nearer the centre of Moscow. We had a lot more Russian servants and spoke Russian at home. Gradually our relatives stopped coming. If they came they were now received in the kitchen. But school was the terrible thing, because now I went to a much grander Russian speaking school. And there nobody spoke to me. The only

---

[3] In order to advance in Russian society and eventually found the credit reference agency that made him rich, Salomon could not remain a Jew. It was against the law for a Jew to be baptised into the Orthodox Church, so he was baptised into the Lutheran church.

girl who did was Stephanie. She was not very bright and had a squint – so nobody spoke to her either.

The second term, when I went back, one of the other girls, Natalia, spoke to me. 'You are not friends with that idiot Stephanie,' she said. Well, of course, I said 'no, never, I've never been friends with her,' hoping to be in with the crowd. And I was. That was when I learnt about betrayal – and I was the one doing the betraying. The other girls did not really like to speak to me because I was Jewish. I denied it, but they knew perfectly well because their mothers told them. At home Mummy became more and more lonely; her old friends could not visit and the Russian ladies never called. Only Daddy was happy: he was getting richer and richer and had plenty of friends. But he entertained them at his club; they never came to our home. Perhaps he was afraid that Mummy would let him down with her Jewish accent. So she had nothing to do except get pregnant. There were eight of us eventually.

Day 4 Moscow 1918, the Witkacy portrait

Bronia is holding the baby under a portrait of herself, as a young woman, done in pastels.

Well, Gervase, this is how I would like to be remembered. It was Moscow in 1918. (The portrait is signed 1917, but that was to protect us; the Bolsheviks did not approve of bourgeois art like portraits.) I was then thirty years old on my passport, (admittedly a false passport and who would put a correct birth date on a false passport?) Witkacy painted me. He had been a handsome officer in the Russian Imperial guard. All the smart ladies had lined up to have their portraits painted by him. That was how he could afford the life of an officer in the Guards. Many of them had, perhaps, hoped that he would do more than just paint their portraits.

Now the boot was truly on the other foot. The Imperial Guard had gone and we had a people's army. Many of the officers had been killed by their men but Witkacy had survived. He had survived, but he looked like he would never be the same man again. He painted me as beautiful, kind and understanding; but this time he was the one hoping to be understood. He talked round and round the subject, but I did not want to encourage him. I had my secrets too; secrets he must not know.

'I was popular with the men,' he said, 'unlike the other officers; I treated them like human beings. That was why they did not kill me.' That may be what the men said, I thought, but the political commissars would have exacted a higher price. The other Guards officers who had survived were in prison, but he was free.

'They took us all to the wood to shoot us,' he said, 'and they gave me a gun.'

'Comrade Witkacy,' the political commissar said, 'you say you are the soldiers' friend, help us to shoot these class oppressors, these officers.'

'I took the gun, but I did not fire at the officers.' (He pauses.) 'What choice did I have, they would have died anyway.'

I did not encourage him to talk any further, nor did I console him.

I left his half-confession hanging in the air. I could see the man had been destroyed and would not recover. I did not want him to elaborate on his confession or bring the whole truth into the open. So that is how I remain on the painting; loving and understanding. But the painting has been battered by life: the chalk is falling off in patches: my expression now has to be guessed. Life has battered my face too. My hair is going gray. These wrinkled cheeks have barely known a smile in the decade between my husband Bolec's death and your birth. So little remains; of all that wealth only this painting and a few jewels. All that remains is the memory of love, love in that same house where Witkacy painted, love of which I could not talk to him because it was not for my husband Leon but for our prisoner Bolec. Because Bolec was under house arrest in our house and I fell in love with him. Bolec's love for me flourished there. He was my prisoner and I was his liberator. He smiled on me and rolled back the horror of the war. He gave me permission to be a private person again. But I will speak of him to you tomorrow.

Day 5 About Bolec (1918-1940)

It is evening in the flat of Bronia's daughter Susanna. Bronia is sitting holding the baby in her arms. There is only one light on. It shows the photo of a military ball.

Gervase, it is time I told you about Bolec; the one whom I loved so long – your grandfather. In that house in Moscow there were three men; the painter Witkacy who came every day to paint me, Leon my first husband and Bolec. Leon was a good and just man; remembering how he died, I will not say any evil about him. We were friends and he was kind to me, but we never had any children.

Bolec was released from prison into our care. He was under house arrest in our house. When Bolec arrived he talked to me so normally, he chatted about the Paris we remembered. You would never have guessed he had just cheated death. He never mentioned prison or torture. He was a short man, no taller than I; but handsome. He was a natural athlete. When he danced he did not tread on your feet; he knew where every part of his body was. Perhaps I should hate him, as people later told me that I should. But I never did; I suffered greatly through him but I knew he would return to me. Together we had the only child he ever had, your mother Susanna; she too inherited his nose. I longed for more children but we were getting older and only miscarriages came.

I've sat us in front of this picture of a ball in Warsaw in 1938, because that is when he came back to us, Susanna and me. That was when he showed his true courage. It was the last ball that his regiment gave for him before we left for Rome, where he had been appointed Polish ambassador to the Italian government. Until then I had never been invited to a regimental ball. Indeed only his closest friends even knew he was married to me. Because, you see, I was of Jewish origin and he was a gentile. But finally he had made public his commitment to me and to the protection of all Jews in Poland. He no longer cared for those like Beck[4] who played with anti-Semitism. So there you can see me in the picture at the ball on his right hand side, looking up at him. He is looking at me, not at other women, not on that night. On his left is our daughter Susanna, who came out into society that night. We were proud of her, so beautiful yet reserved, dancing with grace, but keeping herself free for the career she believed lay ahead of her. In Rome, as the ambassador's wife, I was allowed to be

---

[4] Józef Beck (1894-1944), foreign minister of the Polish government at the time.

his official hostess for the first time. So I am perhaps the only woman to have met both Lenin and Mussolini. But I did not care for them; I only cared for Bolec and I was proud of him.

But in that house in Moscow I was the one he was proud of because I arranged his escape. He was under house arrest in our house. Many people judged me, but I never hesitated. We fell in love, escaped from Moscow, and later married. Palaces and balls have gone, but truth, our truth, remains; a charred seed which will bear fruit in you.

Day 5 The same evening, Bolec (1881-1920)

Gervase, I can see that you are a real boy. You are hungry for facts and tiring already of an old woman's emotions. You want to know a little about your grandfather Bolec. He was born in 1881 at Maksymówka[5], an estate in eastern Galicia, then part of the Austro-Hungarian Empire, and now part of the Ukraine. During his life time it became part of independent Poland. His family were members of the szlachta (gentry) in Poland. The gentry were certainly not all rich; but all were proud and intensely patriotic. It was a much more numerous class than the aristocracy ever were in England. They looked back fervently to the time when each member of the szlachta had a veto in the Parliament of a free and independent Poland. The peasants were mostly Polish, but numerous non-Polish groups lived on Polish territory; Ukrainians, Jews, Germans, Ruthenians, and others. Bolec's father was unusual in that he was not just a landowner, he actually worked. He was a

---

[5] Near the town now called Ivano-Frankivsk but then called Stanisławów.

railway engineer. He built a single-track railway for the Austro-Hungarian government from Tarnów in Poland across the Tatra Mountains to Czech lands This railway saw heavy military use during the First World War. Today the railway only runs to the Spa town of Krynica in Poland; it no longer crosses the Tatra Mountains. The railway ran past the manor house of Bobowa and the Jewish village of Bobowa (Bobov in Yiddish) which was next to it. Bolec's father bought the manor house and built a separate stop for it. The family moved there when Bolec was still young. He had an elder brother called Kazimierz (Kazec)[6] and a sister called Teophila[7]. Bolec was a passable scholar at the middle school in Nowy Sonsz but a wild lad quite out of his parents' control. On one occasion he rode his horse up the main staircase of the manor house, much to his father's consternation. He wanted to be an artist; but his father drove a bargain. If he qualified in medicine in Lwów[8], then he would give him an allowance to study art in Berlin and Paris. And that is what he did. So that he left Lwów a qualified doctor with a special interest in ophthalmology. You must understand that, while Polish was spoken at home, all educated people in Central Europe at that time learnt French as the language of culture in early childhood. German was the language of his education because he grew up in the part of Poland then ruled by Austria-Hungary. In the streets of Bobowa the Jews spoke Yiddish, there was a village of Ruthenians nearby, later he learnt Russian and Italian; his was a multi-lingual childhood and life.

---

[6] Kazek had two marriages, the first to a Viennese aristocrat, and the second to a Polish gypsy. Leszek is the son of second marriage, his daughter is called Dagmara.
[7] Teophila is the mother of Wanda, grandmother of Inca. Bronia had her daughter Susana at 34, Teophila and Wanda had babies in their teens with the result that Inca was only two years younger than Susanna.
[8] Lwów is now called Lviv and is in the Ukraine. It was then called Lemberg in German and Léopol in French.

At Lwów he was the leader of a group of unruly students, but passed his exams. A beautiful bust of him by Stanislaw K. Ostrowski survives from this period[9]. He and Ostrowski were students together. Though they were both to find fame, they were equally unknown at that time. Bolec married Stephania Calvas, an opera singer from a well-connected Polish family. The two went on to Berlin then Paris. They lived the Bohemian life; Wieniawa wanted to become a painter. There is a story that he went to visit Picasso's studio. Picasso was already becoming famous in those days having invented the cubist style. In one corner of the studio, with their backs to the wall, Bolec found a stack of masterpieces in the classical style, which we know today as Picasso's "Période Rose." He asked Picasso about these. Picasso replied: 'when I painted those I was starving; now I can charge £100 for each Cubist painting'. Wieniawa was shocked[10]. Behind his rebellion was a longing to find something completely pure to which he could dedicate his whole life. To supplement his allowance from his father he took some work in an ophthalmology clinic. (Strange as it sounds today, work performed with the hands, such as ophthalmology, was strictly taboo for a szlachta Pole; on the other hand it was acceptable to work as an artist, starve in a garret or be a military officer. They were too proud to earn a living with their hands, except by writing or killing their fellow human-beings.) He took part in "The society of Polish artists", organising fund-raising events and writing the words for a satirical revue performed with puppets, which is remembered in Polish circles to this day. It was at this time that I first saw him, as I told you earlier.

The story is well-known in Poland. Bolec, the wild Bohemian artist,

---

[9] Ostrowski's best–known statue is in Central Park, New York. It is the King Jagiełło Monument which is an equestrian statue of Władysław II Jagiełło King of Poland and Grand Duke of Lithuania.
[10] See sources; Grabska; 'Autour de Bourdelle'

who would obey no-one, suddenly fell under Piłsudski's spell. Piłsudski, who was to be the leader of independent Poland between the wars, was a socialist revolutionary[11]. He had been a comrade of Lenin's brother and at one time robbed a tsarist train of a huge sum of money. He had, however, as he put it himself, come off the train to socialism at the station called Nationalism, Polish nationalism in his case. Piłsudski came to talk to the "Polish artists' society" about fighting for the independence of Poland. Poland was then divided between Russia, Germany and Austria-Hungary. He persuaded some to follow him including your grandfather, Bolec. You need to remember that almost all Bolec's ancestors had died young fighting for the freedom of Poland in various insurrections against the Russians. His engineer father was an exception. Piłsudski was an intrepid and charismatic leader. From that moment Bolec devoted all his energies to military matters. He read military textbooks obtained from his elder brother Kazek, who was an officer in the Austria-Hungarian army. He practised military exercises with his colleagues in semi-secret around Paris. Piłsudski, at that time, headed what would today be called a terrorist group. He co-operated with the early communists, to whom my sister Maria belonged, and whom my first husband Leon Berenson defended in the Tsarist courts. Piłsudski, like me, had personally known the communists early and, like me, he had no illusions about them.

But there is one thing you need to understand about the world Bolec lived in. Once he had married me – and he married me for love – once he had married me, I was invisible. I was not invited to, or received in polite gentile society. The general was invited alone. Most

---

[11] Poland had been partitioned since 1795 between Russia, Germany and Austro-Hungary. It re-emerged as an independent state in 1918, only to be divided again in 1939 when Nazi Germany and the Soviet Union invaded Poland at the start of the Second World War.

of his fellow officers did not know he was married: he was notorious for his affairs, but they were unaware that he was married. Our marriage was legal but it was, as it were, a morganatic marriage; although I was his legitimate wife that did not give me or Susanna, our daughter, the status which he had as a member of the Polish szlachta. Another analogy would be Cinderella in the fairy tale. She was a legitimate sister, but nobody knew of her existence. She gets her prince in the end, and I did too. When Cinderella gets her prince she becomes visible, whereas I became invisible when I married mine. Anyway, I've got a second prince now, and he is quite visible. (She gives the baby an affectionate prod in the ribs.)

Day 6 About spying (1918)

Bronia is playing peek-a-boo with the baby.

Gervase, I know you want to hear about the adventures of spying but first I have to explain why I was willing to run such dangers. I simply wanted a world in which my children could grow up safely. I knew what the Bolsheviks were like, because they had been the clients of my first husband Leon. Unlike most people I had known them personally for years and I knew what murderers they were.

Also, as a Jewish girl I was brought up on the book of Esther which was read every Purim. Esther is called to risk her life for the Jewish people. When Mordechai challenges her to face danger on behalf of the whole Jewish people, she summons up her courage and says, 'If I perish, I perish'. I felt the same myself. After nursing French soldiers all through the First World War, I was not afraid of death; it was familiar to me. Moreover it was chaotic in Moscow in 1918; you could get killed for being Jewish, or being bourgeois. So I thought, 'If I am going to get killed, I'd rather get killed for something worthwhile'.

Then I have a little tip to share with you that may come in useful. I've been through two revolutions; the Bolsheviks, then Mussolini in Italy. The people who come off worst are not those who stand up at the beginning, but those who go along with things until it is too late. The early opponents of Hitler might have spent a year or two in a concentration camp, but they often survived in exile after that. The late opponents had no hope; it was an extermination camp or sudden death for them. So coming out early against the Bolsheviks was safer than going along with them for a while. Indeed, as you can see, I've survived, while my sister Marie, who was a communist, my brothers Guerman, who returned to Russia from France, and Sigismund; they were all killed by Stalin. I was known as Leon Berenson's wife, as a bourgeois wife who would have no sympathy for communism. Although I say it myself, I was very beautiful so those people did not notice me; if I was around, I was invisible to them. They thought I was only interested in smart clothes whereas, actually, I was plotting to kill them all: and I almost succeeded as you will hear.

Day 7 France 1914-1917

Bronia is changing the dressing on the baby's umbilical cord stump. She is tenderly wiping away the blood and pus with some cotton wool, then applying a new dressing. The baby is enjoying all this attention and gurgling with pleasure.

Now, Gervase, you are not ill and this is not hurting you. Nevertheless it reminds me of my nursing in the First World War. I was in Paris, training to be a doctor in 1914. Large numbers of sick soldiers started to appear in the hospitals where we were training. There were far too few French nurses and, frankly, some were not very good. The French government appealed for nurses and I saw that this was something I could do. (My younger sister Paulina, for her part, chose to continue her medical training in Moscow.) Like most of the men and women who fought in that war, I was overwhelmed by the horror of it. We vowed to ourselves that the world would never know another war, but, as you know, our generation was unable to keep that vow.

I was sent to the "Hôtel Continental"[12]. Some, who were not too badly hurt, helped us. They were grateful to be out of the war. Even losing an arm was better than returning to the trenches. Others were obviously dying, groaning and in pain. Sometimes we had very little to help them; one injection of morphine for each of the worst casualties. Often the stock of morphine ran out. The soldiers' agony could be relieved if we held their hands and stroked their arms. But the relief was temporary; as soon as we left the groaning started again. In that mass of humanity it was important not to have favourites, but inevitably there were those with whom we got on better.

That was how I met Pierre Laurent, who will feature so largely in this story. In October 1914 he sustained a compound fracture of his right leg; both tibia and fibula were broken as was the skin. When we

---

[12] At 3 rue de Castiglione, on the corner of the rue de Rivoli. Now the "Westin Paris – Vendôme."

tested his urine it was heavy with protein, a sign that his kidneys were about to fail. But we had a sixth sense about who might survive. Pierre had an intensity, a look of determination which gave us hope. As he improved, I could see that look fixed on me. Because I was so keen that he should get better, because I had spent so many hours dressing his wounds, perhaps I allowed him to hope. But I was already married and Jewish on top of that. I respected his intensity, I felt at home with him when he spoke of books or languages we both knew. But for my part, I never loved him.

Later I got to know his family. His father, like mine, was an immensely rich self-made man. The family were very grateful to me for saving Pierre's life. They took to inviting me to their house in the short intervals between my arduous nursing duties. It was clear that they were willing to overlook any barrier to his happiness. But I never loved him; can we choose whom we love?

Pierre in Russia   Petrograd 1916-17

Exhausted by my nursing I returned to Petrograd and my husband
Leon in 1916. I was numbed by what I had experienced. To be honest
I had almost forgotten about Pierre. He still wrote to me; but I put
him off, as I thought, with polite non-committal letters. So it was a
considerable surprise when, in October 1916, a letter arrived from
Petrograd[13] saying that he was in post there with the French military
mission of General Lavergne. I was torn. On the one hand I did not
want to encourage him. But I could hardly refuse to see a man who
appeared to have crossed a continent at war in order to see me.
Moreover, he made it clear from the letter that he could offer me
action and excitement. I had grown bored of the duties of a wife and
the head of a household. My country, Russia, was going through a
terrible time and I thought I should help.

I received the letter in Yalta, in the Crimea, where I was nursing my
father who was dying of tuberculosis. In November he died. As soon
as he was buried I returned to Petrograd. Pierre was a changed man;
changed for the better. His leg was healed, even if he still limped. If
he was in pain he did not show it. Now he was a man with a purpose;
to prop up the Russian government in its determination to fight
against the Germans. For Germany was the common enemy of
Russia and France and if Russia abandoned the fight France would
face Germany alone. He had learnt Russian perfectly from soldiers
stationed in France[14]. He spoke a rough proletarian Russian like the

---

[13] St Petersburg was called Petrograd from 1914, to avoid the previous German sounding
name. It became Leningrad after Lenin's death and reverted to its original name with the
fall of communism. It was the capital of Russia until the communists moved the capital to
Moscow, in November 1917, after the October revolution.
[14] The Tsarist governments had swapped Russian troops, intended as cannon fodder on the
Western front, for French weapons.

29

common soldiers. This would come in useful to him later on.

I shared his purpose. I knew Russia. I introduced him to friends who, I thought, could help him. He was building a network of informants and writing regular reports back to Paris; reports I helped him to write, about the political situation in Russia. My father's business (the credit reference agency) had also depended on collecting information, admittedly commercial rather than military, so I was in familiar territory. We had been working together for some six months when, in April 1917, the sealed train containing Lenin and the other Bolsheviks arrived in Petrograd. Now I was even more use to him as I could introduce him to the Bolsheviks through my sister Marie. We both knew how determined they were to get Russia out of the war. Indeed that was why the Germans delivered them to Russia in their sealed train. Pierre had tried, but failed, to get the Russian authorities to shoot them as soon as they arrived at the Finland station in Petrograd. We knew that they must be receiving funding from the Germans because of the scale of their activities. We set out to prove this so as to discredit them in the eyes of the Russian people.

Day 8 Petrograd 1917, Bronia as a spy

It is evening; Bronia is again with the baby. Conspiratorially she draws the curtains, leaving the flat in darkness.

Gervase, I promised to tell you how I stole Lenin's telegrams and now I'll tell you. I've drawn the curtains tight, because before you, nobody has ever heard the full story. It is a simple tale of revenge and double-cross – how I revenged myself on Felix Dzerzhinsky.

Felix had founded the Cheka, the first Soviet state security organisation. He had always been a man who loved to wield power over men and women. He had desired power over me for many years, but because I was Leon's wife and Leon was his defender in the Tsarist courts, that made me out of bounds. Naturally, for a man like Felix, out of bounds was all the more tempting.

I was living in Petrograd with Leon. I had been working for Pierre since 1916. Felix used to come regularly for meetings with Leon, who had been his lawyer. I must have been in the room serving tea because I caught the glint in Felix's eye. He'd seen an opportunity to bring me into his net. Could Bronia carry out one simple task for him, he asked. All he needed was for me to receive a telegram and pass it on to him when it arrived. He explained that the party needed a safe middle class address that was above suspicion where the telegrams could be received. They were too sensitive to be delivered straight to Party headquarters where spies for the government might intercept them. (At this stage in the spring of 1917, the provisional government had overthrown the Tsar, but the Bolsheviks had yet to unleash their coup, the coup which would later be called the October revolution.) Telegrams addressed to the Bolshevik headquarters would be read by postal officials: he needed a safe address. I was already working for Pierre so the idea of receiving these telegrams immediately appealed to me. I could read them and pass them over to Pierre before I delivered them to the communists.

'Our address is too well known.' I told Felix, 'I have a better idea.'

'Oh yes, my pretty little head,' he said, 'what is that?'

'Every day I go to my favourite dress shop, Mrs. Tubenthal's. If you use that address it will be above suspicion. Even Princess Lvov[15] uses it. The models who work there receive telegrams from their admirers. Some married women too. There is a silver salver in the models' private room. The telegrams are left there addressed to various pseudonyms. People simply help themselves. No police spies are allowed in there'.

Felix thought for a moment. 'Bronia, that is brilliant. When you have a new telegram put a fresh flower in the window and I'll call as I pass by to pick it up. Nobody will be surprised at me calling here to see my lawyer.'

I could feel his joy at having involved me in his scheme. I could be involved in others and soon, or so he thought, I would be in his power. For my part, although I could see the risk, I felt that because these telegrams were so secret, secret even from his party colleagues, their contents might be interesting. And so it proved. In order to understand our scheme you have to realise that in Petrograd, even during the war, even as the Russian government was collapsing, the wealthy continued to give parties and have balls. It was all they had ever done. Why should they stop now?

But before I tell you about the telegrams I must explain Mrs. Tubenthal's dress shop. Even today I dress well. But in those days I was dazzling. My friends asked me, 'How come you always wear next year's fashion? How can you guess, you who never even read fashion magazines?' Well, you see, Mrs. Tubenthal was my secret. I was very slender then and could wear the clothes worn by the models. The models wore next year's fashion, only once, on the catwalk. The next

---

[15] the wife of the then Prime minister

week I bought it, discreetly, from Mrs. Tubenthal, and as a result I was always a year ahead. Now that is a secret I would not reveal to another woman today, especially not my sisters, but I feel it is safe with you.

Madame Tubenthal's shop was discreet. There was no sign. Only those who knew where it was could go there. A good customer like me could enter the inner sanctum and chat with the models over a biscuit and a cup of tea. If I rifled through the telegrams to pick one for me, people may have thought I had an admirer but that was all.

We collected the telegrams from May 1917 through to July of that year. Then Pierre took them to show them to the ministers of the provisional government. They met, not officially, but in the private residence of Prince Lvov[16]. They could have acted decisively but some ministers spoke against action. In the end nothing happened. When I quizzed Pierre he said that many of them had received German funding in the past; all opposition parties had been funded by the Germans. If they denounced the Bolsheviks, they feared being denounced themselves. Yet I still believe the Russian people would have turned on Lenin if they had known he was receiving German money. Indeed, they did turn on Lenin and he had to flee to Finland for some months. If the full truth had been known, he might never have returned and we would not have had the "October Revolution"[17].

---

[16] On 6/7/17. Prince Lvov was the first head of the provisional government. The better known Kerensky only became Prime Minister later in July 1917.

[17] The October revolution is the name for the revolution by which Lenin and the Bolsheviks seized power. It was indeed in October by the Russian (Julian) calendar used in Russia at the time. In was however on 6-7 November by the Gregorian calendar we use in the West and which Lenin adopted very soon after taking power..

How I freed Bolec 1918

Bronia has set a little table, her sewing table, in front of herself and Gervase. She is going to perform a little play on it for him.

In the winter of 1917, after the Bolsheviks had taken over power in November, Bolec arrived in Petrograd. He had been sent personally by Piłsudski[18]. He was there openly and attached in an informal way to the French mission. Piłsudski had recently refused to raise an army of Poles to fight on the German side, at a famous meeting where Bolec was present. As a result Piłsudski was in good odour with the French and seen as a de facto leader of the Poles, though they were not yet formally independent. So Bolec was present openly but without clear status.

He was a great charmer and got on well with the French. He got on so well that one day Pierre brought him back to our house. I had a salon where the artistic and political personalities of Petrograd met. In Paris I had disliked him, but now we became friends because we had a past in common, and a common goal; defeating the Germans. However no romantic thoughts entered my head at that time; we were both married.

In February 1918, Pierre had to leave for France. I had nursed him through a bad case of diphtheria. The diphtheria anti-serum had saved his life, but not without causing a recurrence of his kidney disease. He returned to France for convalescence. As things became more difficult for the French in Russia, the French military mission

---

[18] Piłsudski was the leader of Poland for much of the period between the wars.

decided to evacuate as a body in April 1918. This was an official train sanctioned by the Soviets and Wieniawa was on it. However the country was chaotic and the train was stopped by Soviet troops near the frontier with Finland. The French diplomats were brought back to Moscow where they were freed. Wieniawa, however, was kept in Taganka prison in Moscow.

At that time I felt for him as a brother. Leon and I tried to free him. This was nothing unusual in Moscow at that time as many people were trying to get their relatives and friends out of one prison or another. For us it was relatively easy as Leon had been Felix Dzerzhinsky's lawyer. We were able to find out where Wieniawa was held. I went to the prison to plead his case[19].

(Bronia plays the scene below to the baby. She uses her two hands as puppets for the two characters. To Yakovleva she gives a harsh, mannish voice.)

Interview between Yakovleva, a female officer in the Cheka and Bronia in the Lubianka headquarters, Moscow 1918. (The Cheka was the first soviet state security organisation, the predecessor of the NKVD, then the KGB. It was founded by Felix Dzerzhinsky.)

Bronia: 'Comrade, I believe you are holding a Polish soldier called Długoszowski.'

Yakovleva: 'I have agreed to see you, but the Party does not recognise you as a person since you are of the wrong class origin.'

---

[19] By this time the Bolsheviks had moved the capital from Petrograd to Moscow. Leon and Bronia had followed the government and were now living in Moscow.

35

Bronia: 'The wrong class origin?'

Yakovleva: 'Yes, you are a bourgeois Jew who has never done a day's work in her life.'

Bronia: 'Is your boss Olga Trotski of the wrong class origin then?'

(Olga Trotski, a senior operative in the Cheka, the sister of Trotski, the Bolshevik commissar for war, was of Jewish origin.)

Silence.

Bronia: 'The man I ask about is a simple Polish soldier.'

Yakovleva looks at a list: 'Yes this soldier is on our list. He was captured in the train of the French Imperialists.'

Bronia: 'Thank you, Comrade, for telling me that he was on the train. Could you tell me where he is held?'

Yakovleva: 'He is held in Taganka prison and he must await revolutionary justice.'

Bronia: 'I know who you are, and I also know the head of your organisation Felix Dzerzhinsky.'

Yakovleva: 'In our organisation there are no heads, we are all comrades.'

Bronia: 'I also know Mrs. Dzerzhinska.' She pauses, 'Does she know how close relationships can be between members of the Cheka?'

Yakovleva (flustered): 'You know Mrs. Dzerzhinska? '

Bronia: 'My husband Leon Berenson is Felix Dzerzhinsky's lawyer.' She pauses.

Bronia: 'A woman can be very forgetful. I only came to ask you for the freedom of Comrade Długoszowski. That is all I am concerned about.'

Yakovleva: 'Comrade Długoszowski is a proletarian soldier?'

Bronia: 'Indeed he is, Comrade, and as an agent of the Bolshevik justice you must release him from prison. He is not a French Imperialist.'

Yakovleva: 'You cannot tell me what to do!'

Bronia, (distractedly): 'A woman can only be so forgetful.'

Yakovleva: 'I will release him from prison because this is the demand of revolutionary justice. However he is to remain under house arrest at your house. If he goes missing you and your husband will be held personally responsible.'

Day 9 Moscow 1918, love

Bronia is changing the baby's nappy. She pricks herself with the nappy pin drawing blood. The blood flows, staining the nappy. She finishes the nappy and puts the baby down. She is in tears.

Dear Gervase, love hurts. There is no way around it. When Bolec first came to the house he was very formal and respectful, a real Polish gentleman. After his time in prison he was thin. He was frightened of sleep; he had to drink every night. Even so we could hear him waking and screaming. What had he experienced in prison that he was unable to forget? Although we were in the house together he only came out to meet me at mealtimes when Leon was there. Yet it was clear to me that I troubled him. He was not used to being rescued; I had rescued him. He was not used to being in debt to someone else; he was in debt to me. He was the Gentile yet I, a Jewess, had rescued him; he was a man and a woman had rescued him. I do not mean that he resented me. He was correct and polite and expressed his gratitude, but his view of the world was being turned on its head. As I see it, this turning from traditional szlachta values, from the values of the Polish gentry, did not reach its conclusion till we reached Rome.

Of course he found me attractive. He was used to women who ran after him, but I paid him no attention, although he was cooped up in our house. He was under house arrest and not allowed to go out of the front door. As my sister Paulina had said in Paris years before, he was the type I most disliked. Yet he was transparently good and I could see that.

We began to talk, first at mealtimes, then in the parlour when Leon was away on business. It was true that we had much in common. We had both lived in Paris before the war; we had read Baudelaire and seen Picasso's paintings. We knew the sorrow and tears of war. We had both studied medicine, although I never qualified and he had barely practised it. But we both understood the body; sweating, bleeding and beautiful. Leon, alas, had an upbringing such that he barely knew that he had a body.

I can remember when we first touched. Bolec was getting very impatient at being under house arrest in our home. I could see that, sooner or later, he would make a run for it. If he did, and I did not distract him, he would put all our lives in danger. So I suggested that he go out for a walk in disguise. The first disguise we hit upon was for him to dress as an ordinary Soviet soldier in a bedraggled uniform. Such men were swarming all over Moscow in those days. Pierre had come back in June 1918 to Russia and had managed to enrol as a Soviet soldier in the Russian army[20]. His mission was to sabotage Russian war material so that it could not fall into German hands. If Pierre could disguise himself as a Russian soldier, so could Bolec, we thought. We found some suitable old clothes, but to complete the picture decided to wind puttees up his legs. He tried to put them on himself, but it had always been done by his batman. So I took over; it was very like wrapping bandages around a leg. Except that when my hands touched his calves, my cheeks blushed. I had to keep my head down and fuss around with his shoes until I had recovered. Of course he noticed. He said nothing but strode out onto the street in his disguise. He was back in five minutes, laughing.

'I heard two soldiers at the street corner,' he said, 'they were saying to one another, 'There goes another Russian nobleman disguised as a Red Army soldier.' Realising the danger he came straight back.

---

[20] Under the false name; 'Piotr Zaitchouv'

Day 10 Moscow 1918, first attempt at escape

Later the same evening. Bronia is feeding the baby with a bottle. Having never fed her own daughter, (a maid had done this for her,) she is inexpert at this. The baby is nervous and cries when the bottle's teat comes away from his mouth. But Bronia is calm.

Don't worry, baby; you'll get all your bottle in the end. Your mother was a worrier and so was Bolec. That day, no sooner had he returned from the street dressed as a soviet soldier than there was a rough knock at the door. Although a man of proven courage in an open fight he panicked, he went pale. I took charge and put him in the wedding chest which we kept in the front hall. He was actually a very short man. I closed the lid and put two precious porcelain vases on it, together with a framed picture of my husband Leon with Dzerzhinsky on the steps of the law courts, standing together after an acquittal. Then I opened the door. The two soldiers who had overheard Bolec stormed in. I could smell the alcohol on their breaths. 'Where is the bourgeois imperialist who came in here,' they cried, 'show him to us and we will not harm you.'

But I managed to look calm. I spoke to them with a steady voice. 'Comrades,' I said, 'there are no bourgeois in this house. My husband is the lawyer for Felix Dzerzhinsky, the head of the Cheka. Do you recognise him on this photograph?' Even drunk, this slowed them in their tracks. 'But we saw him coming in just now,' one of them said. I could tell by his accent that he was a poor Yiddish boy just drafted into the army.

'So if he has just arrived, where have I hidden him? Perhaps in my marriage chest right in the hall? Come up close and look at this photograph of Dzerzhinsky. Do you think he will mind if you ransack his friend's house?' They glanced at one another, suddenly sheepish. 'You report him straightaway if you find him,' they cried, and marched out.

I let Bolec out of the chest. Of course he was grateful and full of admiration for my courage. But his world was being turned upside down again. A woman, a Jewish one at that, had shown bravery when he had panicked. His clothes were covered with dust from the inside of the old chest, so I brushed him down. I removed the puttees from his legs and he disappeared from the room. That evening at supper, somehow neither Bolec nor I felt it necessary to explain to Leon the risks we had run, nor indeed the risk to which we had exposed him.

As the situation in Moscow deteriorated we all three discussed ways of escaping[21]. Certainly if Bolec escaped, then Leon and I would have to escape as well because suspicion would fall on us. Eventually we decided to disguise Bolec as a film actor and this was to work successfully. For Bolec was an actor; he had the good looks, the charm, the immensely charismatic presence, but perhaps also the need for an audience, for beautiful clothes. Like many actors he was at heart a good man.

---

[21] Though they all three escaped, they were to escape separately.

Day 11 Moscow 1918, Bronia's escape

Bronia is holding the baby as she walks up and down the flat. She is restless; the flat is dark and grey.

Dear Gervase, to leave Moscow we had to pack, we had to leave almost everything behind; clothes, furniture, jewels, a great deal of money. For a baby like you leaving is easy. In a few weeks you will leave for Italy on a holiday with your parents and I fear that I will never see you again. But for us it was hard. Russia was my country; I had seen my future there. In my heart I also knew that I was leaving my husband, that good man who had never hurt me. Sometimes in those days, I caught myself wishing that he had died. Every day so many people went missing. A word in the ear of the right person – and they were gone. I was tempted. Though I have never told anyone, I am telling you now. I never did anything but those guilty thoughts haunted me. They helped turn me into the ghost I became during the years in Warsaw.

But to return to the packing; I had to leave all my fine clothes. The false passport I had obtained had me down as a governess. So I packed modestly. No true governess would have been fooled by my suitcase, but the police and customs were. I took no money but I did sew some jewellery into my clothes; gold brooches, a large diamond, ear-rings, and a gold Bréguet watch.

All that remains of my Moscow days is the painting that Witkacy did of me. Witkacy brought it out for me. At that point he was still in favour with the regime. As a painter, taking one extra painting presented no extra risk.

Then we had to pack for my younger brothers and sisters, Roma, Zocia, Adolphe and Vera. For, if I was going, with father dead, they and my mother had to come too. Marie, an active communist, we did not speak to; Paulina, committed to her medical studies, chose to stay as did Sigismund and Guerman equally committed to the law and the air force. How can you explain to children that they can only pack one suitcase, that the rest of their possessions will never be seen again? Of course we lied; we told them we were going on a short holiday to the Baltic coast. I have had to flee twice; from Moscow on this occasion and later from Rome. You leave behind not just your possessions, but also everything you thought you had arranged for the future, the promises you had made, the hopes which you now realised were imaginary.

On that first occasion I did not have time to think, I was running my house and helping mother with her children. Because of her age and her bereavement my mother could not cope. She kept breaking down in tears or spending hours in front of a suitcase unable to pack.

Getting suitable passports was the biggest problem. In some ways mine was easiest because Pierre had arranged the false passport with the French consulate. We had hidden Pierre during his second visit and he more than repaid that debt. He made it clear that the whole family would be looked after when we got to Paris. He obtained false passports not just for me but Roma and Zocia too. Even that ran into problems as the consulate was closed just a few days after I had acquired my passport. The Danes took over French affairs, and they had to add their stamp to my passport.

For mother, Adolphe and Vera we acquired Rumanian passports. Fortunately we still had plenty of money left from Papa's fortune and indeed nothing else to spend it on; we could not take it with us. By this time Russian money was worthless aboard. So it fell to me to visit endless offices that August in Moscow in the heat, carrying large sums of money hidden in my brassiere to bribe Rumanian and Soviet officials. Mother put off going endlessly. Her party left Moscow in September 1919. It took them ten months to cross Russia and reach Odessa. There they boarded a French cruiser which sailed to Paris via Istanbul. Later my sister Marie, the communist, sent us a letter telling us that the police had come and sealed up the house. Was there a triumphant tone in her letter, as we were fleeing and she remained to help build the future? If there was I have long forgiven her, for her own flat was later sealed up by the same police in much more tragic circumstances.

Bronia's false passport
and detail

Day 12 About spying and Bronia's false passport

*Bronia is looking after Gervase while his mother packs. She is in
Susanna and John's flat at 17 Rue Davioud, Paris seizième. She takes
him to a side room to speak to him privately.*

Gervase, the truth is, I could never tell your mother much because
she was such a worrier. Any information I gave her was strictly on a
need to know basis and, of course, she adored her father Bolec. So
how could I talk to her! But with you it is different; your little fingers
curl around my finger whatever I say, and for once in my life I no
longer feel judged. For we, Gervase, you and I, who live between two
races, the Jews and the gentiles, two worlds, the living and the dead,
we are precious people. If both worlds accept us, we can be a link, a
bridge, a place of reconciliation. But when the two worlds are in
conflict, we are the first to suffer. Let there be a declaration of war
and those with one foot in both worlds will be the first in line for the
firing squad.

The dead surround me then as now. All those young men I nursed
in the Great War; many died of their wounds. And how many of my
friends and relatives – not counting Leon, my first husband – have
died in the Warsaw ghetto. As for you, freshly born, you too are a
link with another life, a sign of resurrection.

We people who live in the border regions, we live by smuggling and
spying; the normal rules do not apply to us. What for others is the
illegal crossing of a boundary is for us ordinary life. And so people
come to the borderlands asking for our help; we can guide them
because they are familiar to us.

46

It was the same when Pierre, whom I had nursed back to health in the Great War, wanted someone to spy: he needed somebody who already lived in this border country. So he turned to me. Of course he was already in love with me and maybe that is why he pulled strings to be sent to Russia. But I was keen to help him, as I have said.

(Bronia opens an old leather suitcase and takes out an old passport. It is dry and grey with age. It is dusty, fragile and covered with stamps on both sides.)

Feel this my little Gervase, my old forged passport from spying days. Look it gives my name as Jeanne-Liliane Lalande – a false name. I have not finished with this passport for it will take me on one final journey. Look at all these stamps. The first was made by the French consul. It had all been arranged by military intelligence, but even so we did not quite trust this consul. Indeed the French consulate in Moscow was closed only two weeks later. You can see his bold signature in Cyrillic characters. But he was not a bold man. He was trembling with fear. Pierre and I stood and watched him, we laughed within ourselves at his fear. We should not have laughed so soon. For both of us the youthful confidence eventually went. How could I turn from a youthful adventurer – pursued by three men and desired by more – to a ghost fearful of the shadows that I became in Warsaw?

Day 13 Exile 1918, Aberdeen

Bronia has been rummaging for things in her flat, it is a mess.

Gervase, look at this passport. Can you see this stamp? It reads
'Aliens' office, Aberdeen.' I felt that they had stamped it not just on
my passport, but also on my soul. I had left the country I knew,
Russia, I had left my husband Leon – I was beginning to admit this
to myself – I had left wealth, for what?

When I came off the ship I was surrounded by a great tumult of
people all talking English, a language which I did not understand.
Until then I had heard in the streets of the towns where I had lived
languages which I knew well; Polish, Russian, French, and Yiddish.
It was raining. The granite clad houses looked grey and forbidding.
I left Roma and Vera in the train station; although she was only
twenty, Roma was one of those people who, as we said in the family,
was born sensible. For my part I wandered through the town,
completely disorientated. A kind person from the Jewish
community, perhaps on the lookout for penniless immigrants,
approached me and, speaking in Yiddish, offered me a room for the
night. I started to shout, 'I am a rich, important person, I am a spy
for the French,' but the words could not come out. As I drifted
through the town, on its edge, I found a church. I went in. It was
grey, drab and unadorned. It reminded me of the Lutheran church
in Moscow which we had attended every Sunday. I prayed.

I do not know what I prayed, Gervase, but I prayed. Slowly my spirit
settled. I sat on the hard bench. Words in German came into my
head;

'Zähle die Wege meiner Flucht; fasse meine Tränen in deinen Krug.'

'You have kept count of my wanderings; put my tears in a bottle,' Psalm 56:8; these were words from Luther's bible which we used to sing in church on Sundays.

You must remember that I was born a long time ago. In those days nobody in Moscow doubted the existence of God; he was as real to us as the air or the cold rain. Sometimes people seem to think that because my father had me, a good Jewish girl, baptised at eight, that would have thrown my belief in God into doubt. Not at all, and I can explain it. When I left Russia to study medicine in Paris, suddenly all the inventors of electricity, photography, motorcars and so on, no longer had Russian names but French ones instead. Did that mean that photography did not exist? Equally, to my childish mind, Jews and Christians were both expecting the return of the Messiah. They only differed in one tiny detail; the Jews were expecting a first coming, the Christians a second. But I wisely kept such thoughts to myself.

So I was both a completely religious person, in that I never doubted God's existence, and not religious at all in that I was not interested in the pious side either of churches or synagogues. Nor, and this is a secret for you, was I always sure that all morality applied to me. As I sat in that church my spirit calmed and I set out to return to the train station.

Day 14   Exile, London 1918

Bronia is in the kitchen with her baby grandson. She is preparing a meal.

The big moment, Gervase, was when I got to London. I had arranged for us to stay there with a cousin of Leon's. This cousin was a Lithuanian Jew in the timber business. He sold timber from the Baltic coast to the British market, so that he had an office in London. Bernard was this cousin's name. He wanted to be an art historian like his more famous namesake, the American art historian Bernard Berenson.

This was the address to which Leon, Bolec, and I had agreed to write if we escaped successfully; we had all come by different routes. When I got here, I found two letters waiting for me, one in Leon's careful handwriting and one in Bolec's bold scrawl. As I saw those two letters lying there, that was the moment when I finally admitted to myself the truth about my feelings. Because I put Leon's letter to one side and tore open Bolec's. I so wanted him to be alive. And he was.

As usual he had had some hair-raising adventures. Near the frontier leading from Poland to Russia he and a friend had paid a smuggler to get them across the border. As arranged, they got up early in the morning to meet in the appointed place. Imagine the horror when they found, not the man they had arranged to meet, but his corpse hanging from a tree with a placard round his neck on which was written, 'Death to smugglers!'

They quickly turned back on the road. Fortunately no-one had seen them. They were able to return to Russia and escape another way.

As I read, my heart raced. Later I read Leon's letter. I was pleased that he was alive, but that was all. That evening at table I talked freely about Bolec. Too freely, perhaps, for Bernard said, 'you have not mentioned Leon, yet'. I blushed.

The next day Bernard took me to see the sights of London. We went to the National Gallery in Trafalgar Square. Two painting by Claude Lorrain were hanging in a prominent position by the entrance. Bernard showed me one called 'Echo and Narcissus'. I could hear him jabbering on about composition and form while I remembered the story. Echo was a beautiful nymph who had fallen in love with Narcissus. There was Echo in the front of the picture quite naked, shamelessly offering herself to the gaze of every passer-by. But the only person by whom she wants to be seen, Narcissus, is not looking at her, but absorbed in contemplating his own reflection in the lake. Was Bernard trying to warn me that men like Bolec are only interested in themselves? If he was, I did not want to hear.

Day 15 Exile, boat to Stockholm 1918

The heating in the flat has broken. Bronia is dressed in a greatcoat. Gervase, too, is well covered.

This cold, Gervase, reminds me of my cold journey from Petrograd to Stockholm. Although it was summer, in the second class cabins it was cold. Outside, passing Finnish waters, you could hear gunfire. The Finns were fighting the new Soviet government. Fear kept us warm but once the gunfire had died down, cold crept into our bones. It was also cold because, for the first time ever, I was going into exile.

Until then, my life had been an adventure, full of excitements, but I knew that I could always return to Leon or even my father. Now all that security had been blown away by the revolution. I stayed in my cabin because on the deck another passenger had recognised me as a Moscow Jew and hurled anti-semitic remarks at me, blaming the Jews for the revolution. I was tempted to yell the truth back at him, but in my role as a French governess I pretended to understand nothing. Moreover I had Roma and Zocia in my care. After that I judged it best to keep out of the way.

As I sat there cold in mind and body, I weighed up my options. I realised that I had rather enjoyed the feeling of power that came from having three men courting me; Leon, Bolec and Pierre. But it was time to call a halt. As I summarised it in my mind, it was wealth, glory or honour. Pierre represented wealth; his father was fabulously wealthy. He would inherit the castle at Garaube and much besides. He was a good man and he loved me. Many a nurse has married the patient she has brought back to health. But I could not. I had seen his wounds and they were too severe. Death had been cheated for a while, but it still had its mark on him. I could see it; I think he saw it himself.

Leon represented honour. He was my husband. He had always been kind to me. But I was over thirty now and kindness was not enough. We had had no children. But Bolec, well I only had to look at him and I could see babies.

Day 16 Exile, Paris 1918

Gervase, today I want to talk to you about my arrival in Paris in 1918. I had been in Paris before, but this time I was an exile, with no home or resources of my own. As the steam train snaked into the Gare du Nord, I felt lost. It was true that the Laurent family were waiting for us, but in a way that made it worse. You see, though they loved me and were willing to look after me; they wanted me to marry Pierre, Pierre, whom I had no intention of marrying. Yet I could not tell them too directly because we needed their help.

So if you feel that, unlike other exiles, I had a luxurious welcome, you are right. But I was also rather typical in depending completely on people who had pre-arranged for me a role, indeed a sexual role, which I had not chosen. I met them all. Pierre's father was courteous to me, but very busy, as he had just been put in charge of collecting the German reparations to France. Pierre's brother Jacques was also there, back from the war. Unlike Pierre he had not been wounded. Pierre and I hatched up a plot that, as the younger brother, Jacques should marry my younger sister Zocia. Of course I approved because it meant that the rest of my family would be provided for in Paris. Quite why Jacques fell in with the plan I shall never know. But he not only fell in with it, he fell in love with Zocia. He was in such a hurry to get married that he wanted Zocia to fake her passport and make out she was twenty and not nineteen. I persuaded her that a little waiting would only increase his ardour. In 1919 Babushka (our mother), Adolphe and Vera arrived via Istanbul on fake Rumanian passports, and Zocia could get legally married with maternal permission. So that all the wealth Pierre and I might have had actually went to Jacques and Zocia. I had no regrets on this front either then or later. In my heart I was waiting for Bolec. I returned to Warsaw. I told the Laurent family that I was going to Moscow to try and free my brother Sigismund from the Cheka as I had already freed Bolec. (Sigismund had been arrested by the Cheka eight days after our departure, charged with some of the crimes Pierre and I had committed and condemned to death.) I was able to leave Zocia and Roma with them in Paris. But when I got to Warsaw it became clear that the doors to Russia had been permanently shut. Sigismund's sentence was commuted to imprisonment; he died in the Soviet Gulag[22] in 1937.

But before this could happen I had to be debriefed by the Deuxième Bureau (French military intelligence). For me this was hilarious. There they were, young Frenchmen, questioning me, giving me advice in the minutest detail, when I had for months been risking my life on their behalf. I could barely keep my lips politely closed while I listened to their nonsense. I had brought the telegrams with me in my sewing table. I invited them to find the telegrams. The upper drawer was full of little compartments with needles and so on. One young man pricked his finger, and then got the blood on his immaculate white shirt. The lower drawer was not locked but jammed. They were unable to open it and were about to dismantle the table. I showed them how to do it. The whole upper drawer could be removed as one piece. I turned the table through ninety degrees. A tap, judiciously administered, dislodged the jammed drawer and their telegrams slid out. They offered me further employment, but I declined. I had had enough of danger and I wanted children (she kisses the baby).

---

[22] The Gulag was the name for the vast network of prisons and camps set up in the Soviet Union and described in Alexander Solzhenitsyn's "The Gulag archipelago". There is uncertainty as to the date of his death.

Day 17 A blessing

Bronia is wearing her old paper passport draped like a shawl over her shoulders. She is holding the baby in front of her.

Gervase, today I am going to give you a grandmother's blessing. You've already been christened, so this is a good Jewish blessing. First you have to know the demon from whom I am protecting you. In ancient times in Greece there lived a bandit, called Procustes, who attacked travellers on the road from Athens to Eleusis. He would tie them to an iron bed. If they were too tall, he would cut off the feet. If they were too short he would stretch them out on a rack. Either way they died. So it is with many tyrants, many political systems today. If you do not fit in with their conception of the world, they will force you to fit into it.

That is why I am wearing my old passport. For each stamp – and there are many – is an attempt to make me fit into one of their categories. Some states, like the early Soviet Union, might kill you if, like me, you were of bourgeois origin, a category for which they had no room. Others were less violent. The British simply stamped my passport 'Alien.' But the principle is the same. My blessing is going to save you from the curse of being pigeon-holed. You will notice that this passport, which I am wearing like a prayer shawl, is not in my real name. So, as it was a charm for me, it will be for you. Every time they stamped their marks on it, thinking to limit me to one of their categories, it mocked them because it was a passport which was legitimate but belonged to an imaginary person.

This is my blessing. (She is quiet for a moment.)

When you sit with other people you will always be the outsider. Do not fret about it. Listen to them.

From your point of view you will hear and understand things that they miss. Later you can quietly and simply explain it to them. Say it two or three times. If they do not listen to you, move on.

You will belong to different groups, many at any one time.

Sometimes they will allow you to be a bridge builder. Treasure such times.

At other times, perhaps for many years, you will be ignored. Treasure these times too; fill them with quiet and honourable work.

(She is quiet again, seems to be sleeping.)

(She gets up and walks round the flat with Gervase.)

Let's have some fun now, while your parents are away.

(She pours herself a glass of wine, takes a drink. Then she dips a finger in and lets the baby suck it.)

There you are, be a good boy, have a little sleep for granny.

Day 18 Warsaw 1920

Bronia is showing Gervase two photographs.

Gervase, I am going to describe to you these two photographs, so full of mysteries, and then explain them to you. In the first a young woman, myself in my early thirties, sits in a formal high-backed chair with ornate arms. The room is in the Belweder palace, Piłsudski's residence in Warsaw. The date is early in 1920 during the Polish – Soviet war. Behind the girl is an elaborate arrangement of white flowers that extend from the top of the girl's shoulders to the frame of the picture. Her left hand is dangling on the arm of the chair with the palm turned inwards. As a baby, you will not know this, but this is the pose women adopt, almost unconsciously, when they want people to notice a new engagement or wedding ring. And indeed a ring with a big jewel can be made out on the ring finger.

But why am I sitting alone in the chair? And what are the flowers doing there? The second picture appears to explain the first, but fails to do so. It becomes apparent that the first picture is actually just the left hand side of the larger second photograph. The right half, not previously seen, shows more of the room, though I, Bronia, am still the only occupant. Behind a piece of furniture on the right is a large portrait of a man in military uniform. Who is the man on the portrait, and if it is an engagement or marriage, whose is it?

I know the answer to these questions and I shall tell you. But the haunting sense of these pictures, that of an absence, I did not understand when they were taken, though it soon became all too clear. It is indeed an engagement picture. You may know that my daughter Susanna, your mother, was born on the eleventh of August

Bronia in Belweder palace, Warsaw (early 1920)

1920. At the date this picture was taken, I was already pregnant. That is why I am sitting in a chair with my knees forward; so that the pregnancy is concealed from the camera. When in January 1920 I discovered that I was pregnant I sent Bolec a letter. He was away on campaign with Piłsudski. It was their belief, which I shared, that they were saving Poland from the Bolshevik terror. With great gallantry Bolec sent by return of post an engagement ring and a proposal of marriage. I was delighted. At that time Mme. Piłsudski was a good friend. We were both living in Warsaw. It was her idea to arrange the little ceremony, the flowers, and the photographs, in the Belweder palace where she was living with Piłsudski. Like myself she had been previously married and had had to get a divorce in order to marry Piłsudski. Divorce was not easy in Poland in those days, indeed legally only available to Lutherans. She had had to convert to the Lutheran faith, but fortunately my marriage to Leon had been in a Lutheran church. So Mme. Piłsudski had a fellow feeling for me. The portrait, as you will have guessed, is of Bolec. So that he was present in our engagement. Present and absent as it was to prove to be in our marriage.

Day 19   Kraków 1920, the birth of Susanna

Gervase, I want to talk to you about what was probably the happiest day of my life; the birth of my daughter Susanna on the eleventh of August 1920. In those days mothers who could afford to were delivered at home. But Boleslaw was a doctor and I was a nurse, so we preferred a clinic in Krakow in case of any complications. I was considerably older than most mothers having their first baby at that time. His mother would have had me give birth at their manor house in Bobowa under her care. She explained to us how she had personally delivered a great number of horses, cattle and dogs on the farm...

I chose a Catholic nursing home run by nuns and spent the last month of my pregnancy living there. At this point in my life I formally was a Lutheran. I was happy, if a little bored. Bolec made a lightning visit and, of course, charmed all the nurses.

'We have just won a splendid victory over the Bolsheviks at the Vistula and in memory of that our daughter will be called Victoria,' he announced. The nuns, those most patriotic of Poles, simpered their assent. The name did not please me, but I held my peace[23].

Finally I came into labour. Labour is painful but, unlike the pain I had seen in soldiers dying in the First World War, it had a meaning. I bore it easily; I took pride in refusing all painkillers. I was alone. I had no mother or other relative in Poland. Bolec was still fighting;

---

[23] Moreover, I knew, from friends in the Polish army's code breaking section, that the real reason for the victory was that we had broken the Soviet's military code. The "miracle" was a cover story to hide that fact from the Soviets. Later I learnt that those very code-breakers laid the mathematical foundations for the breaking of German codes in the Second World War.

he was with Piłsudski in Vilnius. His mother was in Bobowa. But I did not feel alone; rather I felt triumphant. At last I had a baby; the child of a man I loved. I knew how much Bolec shared that longing for a child; surely he would never leave me now.

When Susan was finally born the nuns said, 'You must call her Victoria.' It was time for a little play acting. In Poland we celebrate our 'name day'[24] rather as the English celebrate birthdays. I asked the nuns whose 'name day' it was; meaning which Saint in the Catholic calendar had her feast on that day? (Of course I knew the answer.)

'Susanna,' they said.

'What a pity,' I replied, 'when I was a little girl I promised Mary that I would call my first born child after the name of the saint for the day on which she was born.'

'Naturally you must fulfil your vow to Mary, the mother of God.'

And so my daughter was called Susanna, a name acceptable to Jews and gentiles, as well as being in good taste unlike that horrible name Victoria. I did not feel it necessary to explain to the nuns that, at the time of this supposed vow, far from being a good Catholic girl, I was a practising Jewess.

That was the happiest day of my life; until your birth, Gervase, perhaps. But it was also the beginning of my troubles. Because I could have no more children. I fell pregnant again several times, but each time hope turned to disappointment as I had another

---

[24] Imieniny in Polish. 11th August is indeed the Saint's day of Saint Susanna.

61

miscarriage. I loved my daughter, but I doubt if I was a good mother to her. In those days a well-to-do mother had little to do with her children. I did not breastfeed – bottles were the fashionable option then. We engaged a maid to look after her. She had a French nanny from earliest babyhood to teach her French, then the language of culture in Central Europe. When she was four an English nanny was added to the staff so that she could learn that language too. She lacked nothing. Yet she proved difficult to feed. I had to be brought up to the nursery to persuade her. From birth she demanded infinite attention, more than I could give, attention I was not getting myself, so that I gradually withdrew from her. Bolec, on the other hand, Bolec whom she hardly saw, she adored.

Warsaw 1923 Artur Szyk

Bronia is showing Gervase a beautiful page of illumination.

Gervase, can you see the beautiful picture? (The baby gurgles.) It is indeed beautiful. The colours glow and the picture tells a story; a story about a world which no longer exists, the world of the assimilated Jews of Central Europe. In Warsaw in the 1920s there were half a million Jews, almost half the population of the town. Of these Jews many, like me, were assimilated to Polish culture. We had a dual identity as both Jews and Poles. I felt like this and so did the man who made this marvellous print. His name was Artur Szyk. He was a close friend of your grandfather's, whom he regarded as a Polish hero. You can see that the print bears, underneath it, a dedication to Bolec. Szyk had himself fought as a soldier in the First World War and he felt as Polish as the next man. He was not only

"King Casimir III ratifying the "Statutes of Kalisz""
By Artur Szyk (1920)

Bolec's friend but also mine and that was rare. In those times there was a strong taboo against divorce among all Poles, Jews and gentiles alike – and I was divorced. Many Jews never forgave me for abandoning Leon. But Artur was different; he was not only a great artist but a man with a wide heart.

He fought against prejudice and discrimination all his life. In this illumination you can see King Casimir III the Great of Poland ratifying the "Statutes of Kalisz" with the Jews of Poland[25]. You can see the rabbi with the Torah scroll in his hands. In these statutes the Jews were given definite rights. Artur made a whole book of illuminations to celebrate them. In his eyes it showed that the Jews had a long history of relations with the Poles based on legal rights and not violence or charity. Indeed the Polish government of the time agreed. These illuminations were taken on a tour of Polish cities by the government in an effort to promote ethnic harmony.

Gervase, if you look carefully at this illumination with a magnifying glass you will see more. There is a Jewish scribe and a gentile one. The Jewish scribe is wearing a sword; one of the rights of the Jews in the statute was self-defence if they were provoked. This was outstanding at a time when Jews were rarely allowed to bear arms. The Jewish scribe is very like Artur himself, but better looking. If you look closely both the Polish ruler and the Jewish rabbi have two advisers. In each case one of the advisers is looking away

---

[25] The original statutes of Kalisz date from 1264. In painting this scene Szyk, was following a well worn path. In the previous century Maurycy Gottlieb had painted "Casimir the Great granting rights to the Jews of Poland". Before him Alexander Lesser had made a sketch for a similar picture. Maurycy's younger brother Leopold was a lifelong friend of Artur's. Artur, Leopold and Wieniawa all studied art together in Paris before the war. A sketch by Leopold of Wieniawa with Pilsudski is in the author's possession.

distrustfully; it is the leaders who have to bring about this process of reconciliation, they have to lead their reluctant followers.

Artur was physically unimpressive, but he used his pen as a weapon all his life; against Hitler in later years when he was living in America as you shall hear. For him art that did not help people to breathe strangled them. Witkacy, who painted my portrait in Moscow, thought the opposite. For him all life was intolerable, and art was breath itself.

Bronia's story, Bobowa (summer of 1931)

Most of the year we lived in the hunting lodge in Łazienki Park in Warsaw[26], but in the summer we would go to the manor house in Bobowa. The general (Bolec) might join us for the month of August. The walls of the house are thick, exceptionally so. This is because it was built in the sixteenth century by the Unitarians. They were unique among the sects of those days in not believing in the Trinity and in cremating their dead. The ashes they placed in urns deep within the walls; this is said to be why the walls are so thick. On the front Kazek, the general's older brother, separated from his posh Viennese wife, had placed a porch. It was made of concrete, and we hated it. He was so proud of it, however, that we could not tell him. Even in the summer the house was damp. Servant girls from the surrounding farms got up early each morning and lit the stoves. For the bedrooms these could be lit from the outside, so that by the time

---

[26] This was to be near Belweder palace where Pilsudski lived. Wieniawa was responsible for his personal security.

The manor house at Bobowa (circa 1980)

we got up it was warm. You must appreciate that there was neither running water, nor electricity, nor gas.

The whole thing was thoroughly medieval. When Bolec had enlisted as a cavalryman in the First World War, his enrolment papers read, "one man, two horses and his groom", much as the enrolment papers of any of his ancestors in the previous thousand years. The man who had translated Baudelaire's "Les fleurs du mal" into Polish was also a medieval country squire[27].

Near the house was the river Biała (biała means white in Polish). It was a mountain stream which ran over rocks, but with a few pools

---

[27] "Les Fleurs du Mal", or "The Flowers of Evil" in English, was a book of poems thought of as the epitome of mid-nineteenth century Parisian decadence.

where my daughter Susanna and her cousin Inka could swim. Although you might think the home grand, it was not well finished or decorated in the way modern houses are. There were odd gaps between the wall and the ceiling, places where the wind blew in, creakings from floor boards.

Kazek and Bolec's mother ruled the roost and all the servants did exactly as she told them. She was up from dawn, long before us, organising the house and the farm.

Just on the other side of the road is the Catholic Church; it can be seen from my daughter Susanna's bedroom. We could hear the Angelus rung on the bells morning, midday and evening. The Jewish town was a little further away and the women rarely walked as far as our house. They all had red hair, because their heads were shaved when they got married. After that the women wore wigs made of red hair. On a market day the drovers encouraged their donkeys on the path up the hill past the manor house, swearing at them in Yiddish and Polish.

One day the Rabbi Halberstam[28] came to call. He was always polite and relations between him and Kazek were good. As the rabbi and his assistants waited down stairs I was sent to offer them tea. Because of my upbringing I could understand their Yiddish; they presumed that I was of gentile origin and could not. On this occasion I could hear the excitement in their voices. The rabbi's daughter was going to be married. There was going to be the biggest ceremony in Galicia for a generation. Train loads of the Rabbi's followers would come from all over Poland. Quickly I ran to my mother-in-law to warn

---

[28] (Ben Zion Halberstam (1874-1941,)
http://en.wikipedia.org/wiki/Ben_Zion_Halberstam_(I)

her, 'Do not agree to this wedding,' I said, 'it will only bring trouble. With all these Jews staying the local youths are bound to pick a fight'. She looked at me warmly. 'Did I prevent your marriage?' she asked. 'I will certainly not prevent this one. Indeed the way things are going, this may be the last happy day of their lives'[29].

Day 20 Warsaw 1938 The officers' ball

Bronia has put Gervase into his christening gown and is playing with him. She shows him a photograph.

Gervase, I have always loved parties, but this was the best party of my life. It was the goodbye party for Bolec from his regiment. He is at the centre of the group in the picture. All the women are looking at him. I am on his right, Susanna on his left. It was Susanna's first ball, she was eighteen; it was what the English would call 'her coming out'. Years later old men would remember how beautiful she was at that ball.

But for me the significant thing is that I was there. Because after my marriage, although I was Bolec's legitimate wife, I did not venture into gentile society. Most of the officers in the regiment did not even know that I existed. I was Bolec's legitimate wife but my children and I did not get the status of members of the Polish szlachta. Then Piłsudski died and more anti-semitic colonels came into power. Piłsudski death was a great shock to Bolec, who had idolised him. With Prince Cardinal Sapieha, archbishop of Krakow, he had to

---

[29] The bride survived the war and died in London in 2004. Virtually all the Jews of Bobowa were killed by the Nazis during the war; see sources.

The officers' ball (Warsaw 1938)

arrange the funeral in Krakow. When Piłsudski died Bolec's hair went grey overnight. But for me it was a joy because Bolec decided to react against Polish anti-Semitism. With Piłsudski dead he became his own man; it was as if a long adolescence was over. He decided to openly take the side of the Jews who were being increasingly marginalised by the new government.

One day he was sitting in a cafe with Julian Tuwim[30] and one or two other Jewish cronies. He had just come off duty from the regiment. They were eating Viennese pastries and drinking liqueurs. A group

---

[30] Julian Tuwim, of Jewish origin, was perhaps the most famous poet in Poland between the wars. With Jan Lechon and others he founded the "Skamander" group of poets in Warsaw in 1919. He was a close friend of Szyk. Szyk, Tuwim, Jan Lechon and Wieniawa were to meet again in exile in New York in 1941. Szyk became a US citizen. Tuwim returned to communist Poland, where he was named a "state poet" of the regime until he died in 1953. Lechon committed suicide in New York in 1956.

of anti-semitic thugs marched into the cafe. 'Jews out' they called. Bolec drew himself to his full height. (He was very short, but immensely charismatic and everybody knew him.) 'You get out yourselves, before I deal with you as you deserve. And never let me see you in here again'. They looked at each other, hesitated and slunk out.

Bolec's public support for the Jews was why the colonels "kicked him upstairs" to be Polish ambassador to the Italian government in Rome; they wanted him out of the way. It was because of this appointment that he was leaving the regiment and that we had this ball which I am describing.

We danced all night; Susanna with the young officers, myself with Bolec. He was a wonderful dancer. He had a perfect sense of rhythm. You felt you could abandon yourself to him. It was his party, so they chose all his favourite tunes, including the famous 'Uhlan, Uhlan', which he had written for the Polish cavalry in the 1920s.

For years, ever since Susanna's birth, I had loved him even though he had been unfaithful to me. Many people told me to leave him, but I never did. Yes, it was painful at times. But I never doubted my decision and now I had him back. You see I had always loved him. Despite his many faults he was a good man. He married me, when most in his class would have abandoned me. He loved his daughter. He was kind to people and could talk to anyone. Of course when he talked to you, he was completely attentive to you; that was the fascination and the danger.

Bolec as ambassador in Rome (1938)

Day 21 Rome 1938 - June 1940

Gervase is still in his christening gown.

Those were the happiest years of my marriage, the brief years in Rome. I was accepted, I could attend diplomatic functions as the hostess. Bolec acknowledged me in public. Susanna too was happy. We sent her to RADA (Royal Academy of Dramatic Art) in London to prepare for her dream of an acting career. Once Poland had fallen in 1939 Wieniawa really came into his own. He never wavered for a moment in his hope of final victory. Of course Poland had been partitioned twice before and risen again. He wrote all over Europe, wherever Poles were imprisoned. He wrote as if Poland was still standing. As Bolec said, 'all power is an act; it is by pretending that you have it that you exercise it.' At that stage many people were trying to hedge their bets in case the Nazis did not win the war. So he got Poles out of prison or internment; in Romania, Italy and elsewhere. When the Poles were of Jewish origin he was less successful but still wrote and that is what I respected.

He became a close friend of Ciano, the Italian minister for foreign affairs and Mussolini's son-in-law. When Ciano heard that the Luftwaffe was going to switch their bombing from English airfields to London, Ciano told Wieniawa to bring Susanna back from London. Bolec rang her there and told her to come back, but gave no reason. As Susanna tells the story, he had never before asked her to do anything without first giving a reason. Because he gave no reason, she knew it was something important. Those two, Bolec and Susanna, were always close.

We lived in the Caetani palace in Rome in the Via delle Botteghe Oscure. The embassy itself was on the ground floor. We lived above.

The whole palace was filled with grand furniture, Polish paintings, books and other artefacts. Bolec went round the second hand bookshops buying old maps of Poland before the partitions, which he put up on the walls. Because of the war we lost everything. Although Rome was not bombed in the War, one stray bomb did fall on the warehouse where most of our possessions were stored. What remained in the palace went to the new communist government after the war. But I did not miss any of it; I have known both riches and poverty. What matters, Gervase, I can tell you this, is love.

Some people say Bolec was a drunkard and a womanizer. Maybe. But he was mine and he came back to me. In my eyes he was a good man. In the 1930s when Piłsudski started to imprison people without trial, not many perhaps by the standards of the day, Bolec did not want to along with this[31]. Once our daughter Susanna asked him if it was true that Piłsudski was imprisoning people without trial. She was about sixteen. He stood up and began to walk to the door, with his back to her. He said, 'No.' We looked at each other; we both understood that he meant 'Yes', and he hated it. Not long after this incident we heard that Alexander Wat, a friend and the editor of a pro-communist magazine, had been imprisoned. Bolec went to the best store in Warsaw and ordered a hamper of vodka and caviar for Wat and his friends. He had known prison himself in Moscow, of course, and in Germany with Piłsudski. He knew what difference it makes to the prisoner and the guards if they know that the outside world is taking an interest in the prisoner's fate, that he is not just a number[32].

---

[31] In Bereza Kartuska detention camp. It contained about 3000 prisoners.
[32] Wat recounts this episode in his book, "My Century." He contrasts it with the treatment he later received in Soviet prisons.

Day 22 Second exile, America 1940 - 1st July 1942[33]

Gervase, I want my story of exile to prepare you in case it happens to you. Exile is not easy. This is a picture of us on a boat to America, Bolec, your mother Susanna and I. Susanna was cheerful; but not Bolec and I. We put on a front in her presence. Because exile is a game for the young. I had done it once when I was only thirty, but I was over fifty now.

Neither Bolec nor I spoke English; Susanna spoke it perfectly. Neither Bolec nor I would ever speak it fluently. This time I was not going to a lover, but to an unknown country where I had neither friends nor relatives. People wonder why we chose America, but it could not have been simpler. At that moment there were no ships from Portugal going to England, only to America. So we took the boat. We had no money. Bolec charmed his way on board saying that the Polish government in exile would pay once we got to America. They did, but they were not too pleased. Bolec's luck and charm were running out.

On that boat I felt like death warmed up. In my heart I think I could foresee what was to happen. Exile is not for the old. Exiles quarrel, they drink, they commit suicide, as Bolec was to do.

When we arrived in America we had a very cool reception from the consulate in New York. They were not pleased to have to pay the boat fares. Wieniawa, known as Piłsudski's most loyal follower, was yesterday's news. Sikorski and his friends, socialist Poles, some of

---

[33] In June 1940, when it was clear that the Germans had defeated the French, Italy entered the war on the side of the Germans. At that point they ceased to recognise the Polish government in exile and Bolec and his family had to flee.

whom had been imprisoned by Piłsudski, were now in charge. Bolec only longed to serve Poland, indeed die for her if he could, but he was cold shouldered. The ones who were friendly to us were my Jewish friends. Foremost among these was Artur Szyk, the illuminator and cartoonist. As we arrived he was having a show in New York at Knoedler's gallery. This was the top gallery where impressionist paintings were sold to the Clarks[34] and other wealthy American collectors. He got them to employ Susanna. 'She is so young and beautiful, he said, 'you only have to employ her and the pictures will fly off the wall.' And he was right. She was used to entertaining diplomats at the Rome embassy. She could make small talk in four European languages.

Bronia, Bolec and Susanna on board ship to exile in New York (July 1940)

---

[34] The Clark collection of impressionists in Williamstown, MA is one of the largest in the US. His wife was of Polish origin.

The Szyks lived at number two Riverside Drive in New York. They found us an apartment at number three. As Bolec had recognised and befriended Szyk in Poland, so now Szyk looked out for us. Even though Szyk, through his cartoons, was busy alerting the Americans to what Hitler was doing to our fellow Jews in Europe, he made time to help us. Eventually Bolec got a job as the editor of a Polish newspaper in Detroit[35]. This was the longest established Polish paper in the USA with a large circulation among the Polish community. We moved to Detroit leaving Susanna in New York. It was a disaster. Bolec, who had once been able to throw off an article or a poem without thinking, could hardly write a line. He took to drinking heavily again. The Poles quarrelled. They replaced him with a younger man more sympathetic to the Polish government in exile in London. We moved back to New York.

Sikorski, the leader of the government in exile, came to America. He met Bolec. Things seemed to be looking up. He appointed Bolec ambassador to Cuba. It was a small post, but at least he would be serving Poland. But Bolec's friends, the followers of Piłsudski, turned on him. They accused him of betraying their ideals by accepting a job with Sikorski. He was terribly hurt. In his own eyes he was only trying to reconcile people, bring them together. It was too much for his poor old brain.

Don't let your mother know I told you that he killed himself. She's never come to terms with it, for to her Bolec was like God. I too have thought about suicide. Indeed once later I tried to throw myself out of the car when Susanna was driving. Although his death hurt me, I was never tempted to judge, nor was I that surprised. I kept the

---

[35] Dziennik Polski founded 1904.

suicide note; I removed it from the police file. In the note he was still going on about Poland. Sometimes I think he loved Poland too much. He was drunk at the time and threw himself off the building; number three Riverside Drive, New York. What else is there to say...?

But I will pass on to you a debt of gratitude. As soon as we got to New York the Polish exiles turned out to be quarrelsome and unhelpful. Later, after Bolec's death, Szyk and his wife Julia took us in. They looked after Susanna and me for some weeks[36]. I'll give it to Susanna, after the initial shock, she came out fighting.

Bronia bursts into tears. She throws the baby rather roughly onto the bed. The baby starts to howl. Somebody knocks at the door. The door, which is kept unlocked, opens. It is Violaine Hoppenot[37]. She picks up the baby from the bed and walks up and down holding the baby with his head over her shoulder. As she calms the baby, she talks to Bronia.

'Bronia, what is it?'
Silence.

'A man has let you down.'
The tears continue.

'Bolec, it is Bolec you are remembering.'

The sobs quieten.

---

[36] On 2/6/12 I spoke to Alice Szyk, Artur's daughter, born 1922. She confirmed these facts. I phoned her in Florida where at 90 she is still living alone and driving a car.
[37] Violaine Hoppenot had been a secret agent in the Second World War as Bronia in the first. See character list.

She sits and holds Bronia's hand in hers. She strokes it slowly. 'Listen Bronia, he died in the war, just like my boyfriend, Boris. The person responsible is not the soldier who gets shot, but the men who started the war.'

Silence

She strokes Bronia's hand. 'It's Hitler who killed him, just as surely as if he had pulled the trigger.'

Bronia, 'Just as he is responsible for Leon's death[38].'

Violaine, 'And we've got our revenge. Look at this baby. Hitler thought he would annihilate us, but Jewish babies are being born all over Europe, like flowers after rain. We've won. Dry your tears, Bronia.'

'Come help me prepare his bottle.'

Day 23 Bolec's suicide New York, 1st July 1942

Later the same day. Bronia has left the window open and the flat is cold. Snowflakes drift through the window.

Gervase, feel this paper. It is cold. Even when your warm hand gives it life, it is cold. This is Bolec's suicide note. I found it after his death. He'd typed it up on his old Polish typewriter and signed it, as you

---

[38] Leon had died in the Warsaw ghetto in 1941.

can see. He was determined but tired – there's even a spelling mistake in 'Zaponomen', meaning, 'I forget'. I found it at his desk. Susanna never got over that day, and I'm not sure I did. Later we were taken to the police station. Suicide was a crime in the USA in those days. They opened a file and I gave them the suicide note. They got another policeman to solemnly copy it out in long hand on another scrap of paper and put that in the file too. Many policemen in New York in those days were of Polish origin and could just about manage to read and write Polish.

We were called back the next day for further interviews. It became clear to me that things would be easier for the police department if it was not a definite suicide, but a death of unknown cause. While the policemen were out of the office, I opened the file and took out both the suicide note and the copy. I have kept them ever since. If some people do not want to believe that he committed suicide, that suits me fine.

He says in the note that he left us to 'a cold, indifferent world'. But he did not. When he died, and even before, my friends rallied around me. My Russian Jewish friends helped. Of course they had all been exiles and they understood our position. The Poles were a lot less helpful, though Susanna did work in the office of their military mission for a while.

The first and best was Artur Szyk and his family, as I have mentioned [39]. Then Helena Rubinstein employed Susanna in her beauty parlour. Susanna asked her what she should say if the middle-aged Jewish

---

[39] On 31/06/12 I spoke to Alice Szyk, Artur's daughter, now 90 and living in Florida, who confirmed the basic facts.

ladies, who were the customers, wanted to know if the cream worked. 'Look at my skin,' she was to answer, 'I use it every day'. Then Irene Wiley, the wife of the American ambassador to Columbia, John Wiley, took her out to Columbia for a year. Irene was a Russian Jewess like myself. Susanna's job was to keep the ambassador away from the whisky bottle, a job with which she was all too familiar.

When Susanna needed a visa from the Americans to go to Columbia, she had to visit an office in New York. The shy young American boy behind the desk asked her for proof of her existence; a birth certificate, something like that. She maintained that they had all been destroyed in the war. She leaned forward. 'Pinch me', she said, 'I am alive'. He shrunk back. 'Would a letter from my mother suffice?' He agreed to that. I sent her the letter but, made wise by my own passport experiences, made her two years younger. She sent me an indignant telegram, but I telegraphed back; 'You will thank me later'.

Finally there was Alexander Liberman, the art director of Vogue. My friend, of course, was his wife Tatiana, another Russian Jewess like myself. Bolec and I had received Alex and Tatiana in Warsaw, when many people shunned them because she was divorced[40]. Alexander and Tatiana repaid the debt by employing Susanna as a model at Vogue, and later as an assistant in the art department. Finally it was Tatiana who introduced Susanna to friends in the new United Nations interpreter service. There Susanna found her life's work as an interpreter.

---

[40] Tatiana had been Vladimir Mayakovski's great love (Mayakovski was the most famous poet of the Russian revolution). She spurned him for a French count called Du Plessis, whom she had married and then left to marry Alexander Liberman.

80

Susanna finds her vocation; interpreting at the UN (Lake Success 1946)

So you see the world was not as indifferent as Bolec thought; but I bear him no grudge. Like him I have lived a life accustomed to danger, like him I have often thought of suicide. Only you keep me going, and perhaps not for much longer.

(She shivers, gets up and closes the open windows. She wraps Gervase in her shawl.)

Wieniawa's suicide note

'Myśli mi się plączą, łamią jak zapałki jak słoma, zapomonam nazwisk

miejscowości ludzi faktow najbliższych i najpospolitszych z mego życia z historji .. Nie mogę w takim stanie reprezentować nasego rządu ,

bo tylko szkodzić mogłbym Sprawie

Popełniam zbrodnie wobec żony mojej i mej corki zostawiając je same w obcym, obojętnym świecie

Niech Pan Bog zmiłuje się nad niemi

Boże zbaw Polskę

Bolesław'

Literal English translation;

'Thoughts are mixing in my head and break like matchsticks or straw. Because I forget the names of places, people, or the basic facts of my life, I cannot represent the Polish government. I could only cause harm to our cause.
I am committing crimes against my wife and my daughter, leaving them alone in a strange, indifferent world.
May God take care of them.
God save Poland
Bolesław'

(He had just been appointed Polish ambassador to Cuba, but felt that because of his poor memory he could not carry out his duties. He regrets leaving his wife and daughter to the cares of an indifferent world and commends his soul to God.)

Police statement of Roberto Smith 1/7/42

My name is Roberto Smith. I am fifty seven years old. I live at 10 Bronx Avenue, New York. I work as a taxi driver.

On the first of July 1942 I was driving my taxi down Riverside Drive. It was nine o'clock in the morning. I was returning from working all night. I was alone in my taxi and returning home to sleep.

I saw a man in pyjamas on the roof of an apartment block that I now know to be number three Riverside Drive. He approached the railings. He stopped and stared at the sky. The he slowly climbed over the railings. 'Careful, man!' I called out, spontaneously, 'Be careful what you do.'

Of course the man could not hear me. He seemed absent-minded, a simpleton. I saw him put his head down. Then the crumpled figure suddenly dropped. He did not jump. He just fell, as if he was already dead up there.

I stopped my cab and parked it further on. By the time I came back there was already a little knot of people around the body. From that height, he had to be dead, so I did not rush. As you know it is an immigrant quarter and they were talking in many languages, Polish,

I guess, but others too. 'Will anybody call the police?' I asked, but nobody moved. They rather tended to melt away, though others came forward to gawp. So I was the one who left and walked half a block to a public telephone. As you know I was the one to call you. It all took a while. Then I rang my wife Maria at home to say that I would be late.

By the time I got back the scene had changed. A woman in a fur coat was standing by him, screaming. His wife, I assumed. I tried English on her, but no good. So I tried Italian – it was clear she understood it, but she did not calm down. She screamed and shouted, in what language I do not know.

When your colleagues arrived she was suddenly quiet. She told your officers that he must have fallen, that it was an accident. Of course she did not know that I had seen it all. Then the officers tried to question the bystanders, but they all disappeared leaving his wife and me. I feel for the wife, but I have answered all your questions truthfully.

Day 24 About memory

Bronia and the baby are playing with the passport. The baby makes a gurgle which only a grandmother might think was an intelligent comment.

Gervase, you are asking me where my birth certificate, my certificate of baptism into the Lutheran church and all my other papers are. You are not satisfied with the passport. That is very clever of you.

But I never said I would tell you everything. Some things are best forgotten. (Here she makes a movement with her arm as if to sweep away a fly.) Though, as far as those documents you mention are concerned, do you think a French spy, travelling under a false identity, would take her real papers with her? That would be foolish; the papers stayed in Moscow. What did Leon do with them? Destroy them.

You see, Gervase, all this remembering is not as straightforward as it seems. When I was a girl I studied Medicine in Paris. I read the latest philosophers. All girls educated in the French system did. We would talk for hours, often all night. My sister Marie read Lenin. 'Que Faire,' had just been published in French (Что делать? *Shto delat'? In English, 'What is to be done?').* 'The main thing is not to understand the world, but to change it;' that was her motto. I have to say it did not stop her talking as much as the rest of us. Whereas for me the most exciting philosopher was Henri Bergson. He was a leading philosopher of the time and an emancipated Jew like myself. He wrote a book about memory. 'In order to understand, it is necessary to forget,' he wrote. 'He who remembers everything understands nothing.' He gives the example of 'Idiots savants' who can remember everything in great detail, but have a very low intelligence. Whereas to understand is to place the facts in order. The meaning is the main thing, a few facts are gathered around it to point it out and the rest is forgotten. So do not think that I am going to tell you everything I have ever done, I will only tell you those that will help you. The rest – 'bof' – (again she makes a gesture with her hand as if to sweep away a fly).

Day 25 About Bolec

Bronia, distraught, paces up and down the flat.

Gervase, did I need him too much, Bolec I mean, did I drive him away? I had no-one else – no-one in Poland I could talk to; my family were in Moscow and Paris. I needed him, I needed him all day long, and I told him so. I became pregnant several times, but I miscarried. I could have gone out to work, but we had enough money, plenty of servants. As the General's wife, in those days, I could hardly work as a nurse.

He stopped coming home... He would appear the next day, not exactly drunk, but hardly sober. He was never violent or rude to me; perhaps I shouted at him, or clung to him. I knew he had mistresses and it hurt me. Several times I woke to find him gone. On the pillow was a note. He had gone to fight a duel of honour, if he did not return I was to remember that I was his true love. Some husband had challenged him and off he went. Fortunately he was never killed or even wounded. Nor do I think he ever shot to kill or harm. But when I found those notes: what agony in my heart! I would order a taxi and, barely dressed, search the parks and woods around Warsaw. I never found him.

When he came back he would act as if nothing had happened, as if he could not have been killed. For years I kept those wounds to myself, but sometimes the pain just pours out. Yesterday my sister Zocia visited us. I saw you, Gervase, kissing her. I felt jealous. It brought all those emotions back. (She picks up the baby and rocks him. Tears fall down her face. The baby looks, but does not know how to console her. Gradually the tears dry.)

But eventually, as you know Bolec came back to me. He killed himself because his memory was failing. All that drink had softened his brain. Some people said he was becoming an old fool. But I could have looked after him; he was my old fool.

Day 26 About Leon

Bronia has been crying. Her clothes are torn. The windows are open, snow drifts in; it is too cold for a baby.

Gervase, I have just had this letter from Israel. The letter is not signed, but it has the smell of truth. (She lays the letter over the baby's face and is silent for a while.) How he found my address, I do not know. He writes in Polish, but I will translate for you. Perhaps I had hoped Leon might still be alive, that he might not have died, or at least not like this.

She translates;

'Dear lady,

You will wish to know of the death of your husband Leon Berenson. He did alas die in the Ghetto in Warsaw, not by the cruel hand of the Nazis, but from illness and before the worst humiliations were inflicted on us. He died in his own bed of a heart attack in the spring of 1940. Those of us who survived had to forget our principles, but Leon was never brought to that absolute destitution where life can only be retained by compromise. All in the ghetto admired his upright qualities. In the spring of 1940 the head of the Ghetto, Adam

Czerniakow, looked around for an administrator that all could trust. He hit upon your husband. Berenson did not reject this offer out of hand, even though many must have advised him not to deal with such a hated organization. Motivated by duty for his fellow Jews he spent a month investigating the affairs of the Judenrat. He then presented a paper detailing the conditions he would insist upon if he was to serve. Essentially he demanded complete independence; to be the general controller of the whole Judenrat administration. Neither Czerniakow nor the Germans were likely to accept these terms, but fortunately Berenson died in his bed before he was put to the test. As a member of the Jewish Police I organized his funeral. He was buried in the Jewish cemetery and Kaddish was said over the grave of a man who had defied both the Tsarist and Soviet authorities, and was willing to stand up to the Germans.

I write to you in the hope that you will find definite news better than your fears. Perhaps I can justify my own survival to myself if I can bring comfort to some[41].

Bronia puts down the letter. Snow drifts in and settles on her hands and the baby's face.

---

[41] See sources

Day 27 A dream about Paulina

Bronia is more settled. She has tidied the flat and closed the windows. The heating and the lights are on.

Dear Gervase, I had a dream last night. I dreamt about my sisters in Moscow and their children. We have not heard from them since Guerman went back in the 1920s. Simply to receive a letter from abroad is enough to put one's life in danger in Russia these days. So we do not write. But in my heart I still long for them, I was the eldest, a little mother to them. So just before I go, I have been given a dream to re-assure me. The dream was in black and white. At the opening two young schoolgirls are climbing up the stairs in an apartment block, stairs like those 17 Rue Davioud where you live[42]. Although I hear no voice, I know who these girls are; they are Acia and Lily the daughters of Marie, my younger sister, the one who became a communist and worked in Lenin's secretariat. When they reach the door of their flat it is sealed with a wax stamp. There is a poster from the NKVD (Soviet state security) forbidding entry while a criminal case is being investigated. My heart misses a beat as I feel my nieces' anguish; they have been brought up by my sister as model soviet citizens and cannot understand what may have happened to their parents. They go down to the concierge, who appears frightened even to see them and shoos them away. They go to a public telephone and speak to one of their father's sisters. She too sounds frightened. She tells them never to ring again because their phone call puts her own children at risk. Bewildered, cold and hungry, they ring Paulina, Marie's sister. Paulina is unmarried and completely dedicated to her job; she is a TB specialist. She has recently been

---

[42] It was at 8 Serebriany Pereoulok, Moscow.

allowed back to Moscow from exile in Tashkent. When she receives the call, she is not surprised. Even though she knows the risk; exile or prison, she does not hesitate. In a moment she throws her life in the balance. Her voice is firm. She tells the girls to stay where they are near the phone box. She will come directly to them. She arrives and searches the phone boxes until she finds the girls half asleep in the floor of one of them. From that day she brings them up, shouldering this burden as well as her full time post at the hospital. She rarely sees them, but they are secure in her love. The authorities take no action; perhaps Paulina's work is too valuable, perhaps the children's file never reaches the top of the pile, displaced by more urgent matters. As the dream fades, I know that I will not see my sisters again, but Paulina will survive. The two girls will grow up and, after many adventures; these survivors testify to the truth, our truth, about the crimes of Stalin and the other communists[43].

Day 28 Bronia's death 1953

Bronia is ill, staying with her friends the Tubenthals in Paris. She is lying in bed writing a card. She is pale and sweaty. From time to time she lays down the pen as the pain in her right side grips her.

On the card she writes, 'I feel that I have been alone in Paris for a long time. Please kiss the little feet of Catherine and Gervase. Here the heat is tropical – existential. I hope this card will reach its destination, but I fear I will never receive a reply.

Bronia'[44]

---

[43] This dream is based on a film made about Acia and shown on Russian TV. (See Sources).
[44] Translated from the French of the original card by the author.

She is writing to her daughter Susanna who is on holiday in Italy. There is a general strike and neither post nor trains are working, hence her anxiety that she will not receive a reply[45]. And, in fact, she did die before a reply arrived.

In spite of the strike Susanna's husband John, Bronia's son-in-law managed to return to Paris for work, while the rest of the family were stranded in Italy.

As the days passed she got more and more ill. Finally she became bright yellow. A doctor was called in. Because it was August all the regular doctors were on holiday so that he was a young and inexperienced locum. He felt that he needed the permission of a relative before he transferred her to a private clinic. We can suppose that Bronia was reluctant to go. As soon as John returned he found a card under his doormat urgently requiring his help. He took a taxi to the Tubenthals' flat and arranged for her immediate admission.

By then she was very ill. They operated that night and removed a stone from her bile duct. Because of her fever they gave her penicillin but the infection did not respond and she died three days later. (Only plain penicillin was available in 1953; penicillin derivatives effective against biliary sepsis were not discovered until later.)

Since John could not contact his wife, stranded in Italy, he had to arrange the funeral himself. He was able to do this with great tact. This endeared him to the French family who thereafter regarded him as a proper English gentleman. He arranged for her to be buried in

---

[45] http://fr.wikipedia.org/wiki/1953_en_France

the Laurent family tomb in the 'Cimetière de Montparnasse.' She was buried under the name 'Jeanne Lalande,' which she had first used as a French spy in Petrograd in 1916. In this way she remained as discreet in death as she had been in life. Apart from her son-in-law, there were three sisters at the funeral; Zocia, who had married Jacques Laurent, Pierre's younger brother, Roma, an Orthodox nun[46], and Vera who worked as a translator. Adolphe, who was in the late stages of chronic schizophrenia, was alive, but never left Vera's flat. Babushka, Bronia's mother, had survived the German occupation of France, but died in 1944. Unbeknown to them all Paulina was still alive and working as a doctor in Moscow. Marie, Zigismund and Guerman died in Stalin's purges. Paulina, at considerable risk to herself, had brought up Marie's two daughters, Acia and Lily. After 1970 the families found each other and were reunited. Blood had proved stronger than communism. As Paulina came off the plane in Paris she and Vera greeted each other by immediately launching into an argument they had failed to finish when they parted half a century earlier.

---

[46] Roma was a nun according to my father; I think he referred to a devout way of life rather than formal vows.

Timeline for the life of Bronia

	Bronia	Bolec	Wars	Political events
1881		Birth		Poland partitoned between Russia, Germany and Russia since 1795
1886	Birth			
1902	Baptised Lutheran			
1909	Marries Leon			
1914	Nursing in Paris	Joins Pilsudski's legions	WW1 starts	
1916	Returns to Russia, Spying	Imprisoned in Magdeburg fortress with Pilsudski		
1918	Escape from Moscow	Escape from Moscow	WW1 ends	Bolshevik revolution
1920	Birth of daughter		Polish-Soviet war (1919-1921)	Second Polish Republic (1918-1939)
1938		Appointed Polish ambassador to Rome		
1939			WW2 starts	Poland invaded by the Germans from the West and Russians from the East
1940	Flees Rome for exile in New York	Flees Rome for exile in New York	Italy, initially neutral, enters WW2	
1942		Death		
1945			WW2 ends	
1949	Marriage of daughter Susanna			
1953	Birth of grandson Bronia's Death			

Sources

For General Bolesław Wieniawa Długoszowski;

http://en.wikipedia.org/wiki/Boles%C5%82aw_Wieniawa-
D%C5%82ugoszowski
Originally written by the author almost twenty years ago, but much vandalized.

http://pl.wikipedia.org/wiki/Boles%C5%82aw_Wieniawa-
D%C5%82ugoszowski
The polish site; more extensive, but no mention of his second wife. This is the source for the 'Roberto Smith' letter.

http://it.wikipedia.org/wiki/Boles%C5%82aw_Wieniawa-
D%C5%82ugoszowski
The Italian site, highly inaccurate.

http://www.youtube.com/watch?v=jNalHMg3A2c
This leads to a half hour film about Wieniawa. The principal talking head is his daughter Susanna.

Bialwasiewicz W. Amarant na bruku (an article about Wieniawa). Aksent 1985;2-3(20-21):138-49.

Dworzynski W. Wieniawa poeta, żolnierz, dyplomata. Wyd. 1 ed. Warszawa: Wydawnictwa Szkolne i Pedagogiczne; 1993.

Garnier J-P. A Varsovie sous Piłsudski. La Revue des Deux Mondes 1960 Dec 15;24(3):643-5.

Grabska-Wallis E, Pytasz M. Szuflada generala Wieniawy wiersze i dokumenty : materiały do twórczości i biografii Bolesława Wieniawy-Długoszowskiego. Warszawa: Państwowy Instytut Wydawniczy; 1998.

Grabska-Wallis E (Ed.) Autour de Bourdelle, Paris et les artistes Polonais 1900-1918. Paris: Paris Musèes; 1996. Page25 is a French translation of a

94

previously unpublished fragment by Wieniawa telling the story of his vist to Picasso. The whole book an essential source for his French period.

Grochowalski W. Ku chwale Wieniawy w 120 rocznicę urodzin. Lodsz: Wydawn. Papier-Service; 2001.

Hubiak Piotr. Belina i jego ułani. Krakow BCDCN 2003

Majchrowski J. Ulubieniec cezara Boleslaw Wieniawa- Długoszowski: zarys biografii. Wrocław: Zakład Narodowy im. Ossolińskich; 1990. (The most acurate according to my mother)

Majchrowski J. Pierwszy ulan Drugiej Rzeczypospolitej. Wyd. 1 ed. Warszawa: Polska Oficyna Wydawnicza "BGW"; 1993.

Pioro, T. Unplished fragment in French, presumably intended as a newspaper article in France. Probably 1930s. In the author's possesion. (This is the source of the name "Yakovleva".)

Romański R. General Bolesław Wieniawa- Długoszowski polityk czy lew salonowy? Warszawa: Bellona; 2011.

Strzalka K. Meetings of Boleslaw Wieniawa-Dlugoszowski and Galeazzo Ciano in 1939-1940. The Polish Quarterly of International Affairs 2007;(3):88-123. (The best source for Wieniawa's activity in Rome after the fall of Poland.)

Urbanek M. Wieniawa - szwolezer na pegazie. Wroclaw: Wydaw. Dolnośląskie; 1991.

Wat, Alexander. My Century. New York Revue of Books Classic. New York. 2003

Wieniawa- Długoszowski i B, Grochowalski W. Wiersze i piosenki. Lodz: "Papier-Service"; 2002.

Wieniawa Długoszowski i B, Loth R. Wymarsz i inne wspomnienia. t. 75 ed. Warszawa: Biblioteka "WiŽTzi"; 1992.

Wieniawa- Długoszowski B. Księga jazdy polskiej. Warszawa: Wydawn. Bellona; 1993.

Wittlin T. Szabla i kon. Londyn: Polska Fundacja Kulturalna; 1996.

Wolos Mariusz. General dywizji Bolesław Wieniawa- Długoszowski Biografia wojskowa. Torun. Wydawnyctwo Adam Marszałek; 2000.

For Bronisława Wieniawa Długoszowska;

False passport, referred to in the text and other papers in the possession of the author

Garnier J-P. A Varsovie sous Piłsudski. La Revue des Deux Mondes 1960 Dec 15;24(3):643-5.

(origin of "like a ghost" in Warsaw between the wars)

François Garnier. 'Pierre Laurent'; Paris; July 1998 (see below). This is the only source we have for her birth date.

Portrait by Witkacy, Moscow 1917 (frontispiece)

Alexander Lauterbach, a Polish Jew born in the 1920s, who escaped during the war and later married into the Szyk family has read and corrected the manuscript. He suggests that the Kliatchkin family would have more likely spoken Polish at home, not Yiddish, before the move to Moscow. A typescript of his life is in the author's possesion.

For Kazimierz Wieniawa Długoszowski;

Skotnicki A, Klimczak W. Jewish Society in poland. Krakow: Widawnictwo AA; 2009.

The picture on the front is Kazek with the Bobover Rebbe.

For Irena (Inka) Bokiewicz (cousin of Susanna);

Wojtek the bear, hero of World War Two. Orr,Eileen. Birlinn Ltd. 2012

DVD "Wojtek, the bear that went to war." BBC Scotland 2011. www.wojtekfilm.com

Inka was the young Pole who bought Wojtek as a baby bear in the mountains of Iran. She appears in the documentary.

For Susanna Vernon;

http://downloads.unmultimedia.org/photo/medium/189/189118.jpg

A picture of her as one of the first simultaneous interpreters at the UN (Lake success, New York) in 1948.

For Leon Berenson;

http://pl.wikipedia.org/wiki/Leon_Berenson

Okrét Leon. Między życiem a sądem. Institut Wyd. 'Renaissance'. Warsaw.1938. A book of reminiscences about lawyers and famous cases in Warsaw in the 1920s, with an introduction by Leon Berenson.

Kassow notes that Ringelblum "endorsed the proposal by the noted attorney Leon Berenson for a post-war monument to the "unknown smuggler.""

Kassow S. Who will write our history? London: Penguin books; 2007.

Ringelblum E. Notes from the Warsaw Ghetto. New York: Ibooks incorporated; 2006.

For his death;

Barbara Engelking, Jacek Leociak. "The Warsaw Ghetto" Yale University Press, New Haven, 2009, p.157. On p.542 it is stated that he wrote a record of his experiences, which has been lost. Another version to be found on the internet has Berenson considered for the role of head of the Jewish police, not the whole Judenrat administration.

For his gravestone at the Jewish cemetery in Okopowa Street in Warsaw; **http://pl.wikipedia.org/w/index.php?title=Plik:Leon_Berenson_5.JPG& filetimestamp=20080603223045**

For a picture; "Warsaw lawyers in the 1920s," he is the one in the middle.
http://en.korbonski.ipn.gov.pl/dokumenty/zalaczniki/14/14-21776.jpg

For Pierre Laurent;

François Garnier. 'Pierre Laurent'; Paris; July 1998, (self published, in the possession of the author). François Garnier is the husband of Jacqueline, the eldest of Jacques and Zocia's daughters.

For Charles Laurent;

http://fr.wikipedia.org/wiki/Charles_Laurent

For the Jews of Bobowa (Bobov);

Skotnicki A, Klimczak W. Jewish Society in poland. Krakow: Widawnictwo AA; 2009.

The picture on the front is Kazek with the Bobover Rebbe. The marriage of the Rebbe's daughter is on p.21-29, p51-56 covers Bobowa during the German occupation, etc.

Oliner S. Restless Memories; Recollections of the holocaust years. Berkeley, California: Judah L. Magnes Museum; 1986. (A moving account by one of the three known survivors of the final liquidation of the Bobowa ghetto. He later became a distinguished professor of sociology. He wrote exentisevly about altruism and the holocaust. He describes how the last Jews of Bobowa were deported, not to Auchwitz, but to a nearby forest called Garbacz, where they were shot.)

Garbacz is near Stróżówka village, Gorlice. After the war a memorial was set up there;
http://www.sztetl.org.pl/en/article/gorlice/13,places-of-martyrology/1117,the-mass-grave-in-the-garbacz-forest/

Gliksman, Devora. Nor the moon by night; the survival of the Chassidic dynasty of Bobov. Jerusalem/New York; Feldheim publishers; 1997

Gilbert, Martin. The boys triumph over adversity. London. Wiedenfeld and Nicholson. 1996

Ben Zion Halberstam (1874-1941,)
http://en.wikipedia.org/wiki/Ben_Zion_Halberstam_(I)
For the marriage of the rabbi's daughter see;
http://www.sztetl.org.pl/en/article/bobowa/5,history/

Majcher, Karol. Bobowa historia, ludzie, zabitki. Bobowa. 1991.
For Witkacy;

http://en.wikipedia.org/wiki/Stanis%C5%82aw_Ignacy_Witkiewicz
Edited and translated by Gerould, Daniel. The Witkiewicz reader.
London. 1993. Quartet books.

For Szyk;

http://en.wikipedia.org/wiki/Arthur_Szyk

Ansell, Joseph. Arthur Szyk, artist, Jew, Pole. Oxford. The Littman library of Jewish Civilisation. 2004. The illumination referred to in the text is plate number 12 in this book.

For Dzerzhinsky;

http://en.wikipedia.org/wiki/Felix_Dzerzhinsky

For Salomon Kliatchkin;

S. G. Kliatchkine 'Activités des services de renseignements sur la solvabilité en matière de crédit en Russie.' Moscow c. 1910. (In the author's possession.) At that time "S. G. Kliatchkine et Cie." the first credit reference agency in Tsarist Russia, had a building in Red Square, where it makes a corner with one of the principal avenues. The building still stands. The credit reference agency employed about 200 people.

La famille Kliatchkine. Eighteen pages of handwritten notes by Vera Kliatchkin. Undated. Highly unreliable.

According to Vera; Bronia, finished lycée in 1903 with gold medal, went to Paris to study medicine, returned to Moscow 1909 to marry Leon Berenson, unconsummated marriage, he living in Warsaw and she in Paris, finished medical studies but did not "defend her thesis". She states that Adolphe never learnt French properly. He speculated successfully in foreign currency in Berlin 1914-1924 then moved to Paris and "went into a decline". He may have suffered from schizophrenia. From 1959 he lived in Vera's flat and she looked after him. She was to suffer from the same illness towards the end of her own life.

For Violaine Hoppenot;

http://biwako.skynetblogs.be/archive/2008/06/14/seul-entre-meuse-et-ourthe-boncelles-tient.html

Claudel, Paul (Texte) Hoppenot, Helene (Photographies). La Chine. Geneva. Albert Skira. 1946. A copy of this book by Violaine's mother Helene, inscribed by Violaine, Geneva 1950, was formerly in the possession of the family.

For Marie, Paulina, Acia and Lily;

http://iconotheque-russe.ehess.fr/film/1034/

Film shown on Russian television 2008 "The history of a family who witnessed an epoch". A film by Svetlana Tandit. OOO "CM Film", Russia, 2008. The life of Assia and the Kliatchkin family in Stalin's Russia. (Video and transcript in the author's possession.)

Printed in Great Britain
by Amazon.co.uk, Ltd.,
Marston Gate.